The Monticello Baby Miracles

Double bundles of joy!

Twin sisters spontaneous Claudia and reserved
Harriet might be chalk and cheese, but no matter
the distance between them, they are each other's best
friend. And then they both get news that will change
their lives forever!

For the Monticello sisters, it seems miracles will
always come in twos…

Read Harriet's story in
One Night, Twin Consequences
by Annie O'Neil

An invitation from the delectable Dr. Matteo Torres
to work with orphans in Argentina is a dream come
true for Harriet. It's also right out of her comfort
zone! And then one night of seduction leads to a *very*
unexpected consequence and double the trouble!

and

Read Claudia's story in
Twin Surprise for the Single Doc
by Susanne Hampton

Claudia Monticello must accept former obstetrician
Patrick Spencer's help when she goes into labor in a
broken elevator! But after seeing her sons in gorgeous
Patrick's arms, Claudia finds herself hoping this
handsome stranger might just be the daddy her little
family needs!

Both available now!

Dear Reader,

Claudia Monticello has accepted that she's more like her fiery, impulsive Italian father than her sweet and sensible Irish mother. The "sensible" genes have been lavishly bestowed upon her twin sister, Harriet. But she also knows that her impulsive decisions and her desire to take everyone at face value—particularly men—have to stop. Her need to live life to the fullest has led her to the other side of the world on not much more than a whim—and that's the *least* serious of the repercussions!

Claudia has received life-changing news and she realizes she has no choice but to be responsible. And suddenly—and surprisingly—that doesn't seem so hard. Her heart is already consumed with love for her unborn babies, and their needs will forevermore come first. The only men who have a future in her life are her two sons.

That is until she meets Dr. Patrick Spencer.

This former obstetrician has left his life in London to start a new life in Los Angeles. But the disappointment that has driven him five thousand miles from home seems to follow him and, despite a new career, he never feels fulfilled.

That is until he meets Claudia Monticello.

They have both left London for very different reasons, but when their worlds collide, they are forced to question their decisions never to love again.

I hope you enjoy Claudia and Patrick's journey to happily-ever-after. It's a bumpy ride, so you might need to hold on tight…just as tightly as my hero and heroine do from the moment they meet!

Warmest regards,

Susanne

TWIN SURPRISE FOR THE SINGLE DOC

—

SUSANNE HAMPTON

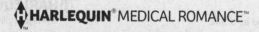

HARLEQUIN® MEDICAL ROMANCE™

Recycling programs
for this product may
not exist in your area.

ISBN-13: 978-0-373-01116-2

Twin Surprise for the Single Doc

First North American Publication 2016

Copyright © 2016 by Susanne Panagaris

Printed in U.S.A.

www.Harlequin.com

Books by Susanne Hampton

Harlequin Medical Romance

Midwives On-Call
Midwife's Baby Bump

Unlocking the Doctor's Heart
Back in Her Husband's Arms
Falling for Dr. December
A Baby to Bind Them
A Mommy to Make Christmas

Visit the Author Profile page
at Harlequin.com for more titles.

To everyone who thought they had closed their hearts to love…only to be proved wrong by a love stronger than the heartache they had survived.

And to Alli and Gilda and all of my amazing friends who constantly provide inspiration for my books.

Praise for
Susanne Hampton

"A stunning read about new beginnings that is guaranteed to melt any reader's heart."

—*Goodreads* on
Falling for Dr. December

"Probably one of my top ten favorite reads this year. It was heartbreaking…kept me wanting to read to find out what happens next."

—*Goodreads* on
A Baby to Bind Them

"I truly enjoyed this book. It was such a stunning emotional rollercoaster of a read it tugged on all the right heartstrings to bring me tears of joy and sadness."

—*Contemporary Romance Reviews* on
Unlocking the Doctor's Heart

CHAPTER ONE

'CONGRATULATIONS, CLAUDIA. You're having twins!'

Claudia Monticello's deep brown eyes, inherited from her Italian father, widened like dollhouse-sized plates against her alabaster skin, a present from her Irish mother. In a rush of panic and disbelief, her gaze darted from the gel-covered bump of her stomach to the grainy black-and-white images on the screen, then to the *pleased as punch* radiologist's face before finally looking up to the ceiling to where she imagined heaven might be. Not that she thought her parents would be smiling down at her after what she had done.

Suddenly the room became very hot and she struggled a little to breathe. The clammy fingers of one hand reached for the sides of the examination table to steady herself. *Two babies*. Her mouth had dropped open slightly, but her lips had not curved to anything close to a smile. In denial, she shook her head from side to side and nervously chewed on the nails of the other hand. There had to be a mistake. The radiologist, still smiling at the screen and apparently unaware of the panic blanketing her patient, gently moved the hand piece over Claudia's stomach to capture additional images.

She must have zoomed in too quickly, Claudia mused.

Double imaged.

Misread the data.

Be new at her job.

But Claudia knew without doubt, as she slowly and purposefully focused on the screen, there was no mistake. There were two tiny babies with two distinct heartbeats. The radiologist was using her finger to point to them. Her excitement was palpable. A reaction juxtaposed to Claudia's. At twenty-nine years of age, Claudia Monticello was anything but excited to be the single mother of twins. For many reasons… The first was her living five thousand miles from home…and the second was the fact her children would never meet their father.

* * *

Twenty weeks had passed since Claudia discovered she was to be the mother of two and, as she dropped her chin and looked down at her ample midsection while waiting for the elevator, she was pleased to see they were healthy-sized babies. Her waist was somewhere hidden underneath her forty-five-inch circumference and she hadn't seen her ankles for weeks. Her mood was one of anticipation as she waited for the doors to open on her floor. Her final obstetric visit was imminent and she was thinking about little else than her flight home to London the next day. It couldn't come quickly enough for her. She couldn't wait to farewell Los Angeles.

And turn her back on the disappointment and heartache the city had brought.

Or, more correctly, that she had invited into her life.

The day was warm and she was wearing a sleeveless floral maternity dress, one of three she'd picked up on the sale rack in Macy's when she rapidly outgrew all her other clothes, flat white sandals and her oversized camel-coloured handbag that she took everywhere. Her deep chocolate curls were short and framed her pretty face, but her eyes were filled with sadness. She pictured her suitcases, packed and waiting just inside the door of her apartment. She was finally leaving the place she had called home for almost a year. The fully furnished apartment was in a prime high-rise gated community on Wilshire Boulevard and in demand. The home would have new tenants within days. It had only been temporary, like so much in that town, and she wondered who would be sleeping in the king-sized bed later that week and what the future held for them. She hoped for their sake they hadn't rushed into something they would live to regret.

The way she had.

Patrick Spencer waited inside the elevator for the doors to open. It had only managed to travel down one floor and was already stopping. A sigh escaped from his lips. He prayed it wouldn't stop on every floor on the way to street level. His patience was already tested. He was having another one of those days. A day when he felt frustrated with life and struggled with a cocktail of resentment mixed with equal parts of doubt and disappointment and a dash of boredom with his new reality. Not that his reality was devoid of life's luxuries, but it was missing the passion he'd once felt. It was another day when he felt cheated out of what he had planned and wanted for his future, even though he was the one who'd walked away from everything. A day when he almost didn't give a damn. And whenever he had those days he always put on his sunglasses and tried to block out the world in which he lived. He had been cornered into this new life. That was how he saw it.

If things had not gone so terribly wrong, he would be living in London instead of calling Los Angeles home.

With melancholy colouring her mood, Claudia paid little attention to the tall, darkly dressed figure when she stepped into the elevator. But she noticed the affected way he was wearing wraparound sunglasses with his suit. It was more of the same pretentious LA behaviour.

Sunglasses inside an elevator? In Claudia's sadly tainted opinion, all men were hiding something; perhaps this one was nursing a hangover. She rolled her eyes, confident in the fact he couldn't see anything from behind the dark lenses and even more sure he wouldn't be looking in her direction anyway. Probably obsessed with his own thoughts and problems. Just like so many in this town. A town full of actors, many with an inflated sense of self-worth and a complete lack of morals. Perhaps this man filled that same bill, she surmised. She felt sick to her stomach even thinking about the man who had wooed her with lies and then walked out of her life as shamelessly as he had walked into it.

She patted her stomach protectively and, not caring a damn what he thought, she whispered, 'You may have been a surprise, boys, but I love you both to the moon and back already.' Then she silently added, *And I will make sure you don't run away from your responsibilities...or wear sunglasses in a lift!*

'They're very lucky little boys.' Patrick said it matter-of-factly. It surprised even him that he had made a comment but hearing the woman speak so genuinely to her unborn children in an accent once so familiar struck a chord with him. In a town so devoid of anything genuine, Patrick felt compelled to comment.

Claudia thought for a fleeting moment his words had been delivered with genuine sentiment. But her body stiffened as she reminded herself there was little or no sentiment in that town. Maternal hormones, she assumed, had temporarily dressed her vision with rose-coloured glasses. His English accent, for some reason, made her drop her guard just a little. Against her better judgement, she looked over to see the man remove his sunglasses. His lips were curved slightly. Not to a full smile, not even a half smile, but she could see his teeth just a little. They were almost perfect but not veneer flawless.

He was tall, six foot one or two, she guessed, as she was five foot nine in bare feet or the flat shoes she was wearing that day. He was broad-shouldered and, she imagined from the way his shirt fell, buff, but he wasn't overly tanned. His hair was short and light brown in colour and it was matched with a light covering of stubble on his face. His grooming was impeccable but, aside from the stubble, quite conservative. While his looks, she conceded, were worthy of a billboard, his styling was more professional than the usual LA playboy slash actor type. Or, in his case, an English ex-pat playing the LA field.

'I'm sorry?' she finally said after her assessment. She was hoping he would shrug his shoulders, put his sunglasses back on and return to thoughts of himself or his most recent conquest.

But he didn't.

'I said that your babies are very fortunate that you care for them so much even before they enter the world. I hope they make you proud.'

Patrick had not said anything like that in twelve years. They were words he used to say every day as a matter of routine, but never so routine that they were not sincere. But something about this woman and the palpable love he could see in her eyes and hear in her voice made it impossible not to make comment. She appeared different from the women he knew.

And a very long way from the women he bedded. She was cute and beautiful, not unlike a china doll. His women were not fragile like that.

And her love for her unborn children was special. It was something Patrick very much appreciated.

Claudia felt her stance stiffen again and her expression become quite strained. His accent was cultured and, with her own English upbringing and resultant class-consciousness, she suspected he had more than likely experienced a privileged boarding school education. His clothes were high end designer. She knew he must have an ulterior motive. All men did. There were a handful of people she had met in the year since she'd left London to make Hollywood her home who had shown a level of genuine kindness but she doubted this man would join those ranks. In fact, she doubted that any man would ever again join that group. Her desired demeanour was defensive and with little effort she reached it. No man was going to get within a mile of her or, more particularly, her children with any line. She had told herself that she had finished with men and all of their agendas. And she decided to prove it to herself.

Her first step would be keeping this man, albeit a very attractive man, at arm's length. Perhaps even offside.

'You really should refrain from eavesdropping; it's rude,' she said before turning her attention back to the blank gunmetal doors. *There—it was done!* She had stood up for herself and it brought her a sense of empowerment.

It had been a long time coming and she conceded her ire was directed towards the wrong man but she had finally felt strong enough to say something. And it felt good. As if she was claiming her power back.

But the elevator didn't feel good or seem to have any power. It seemed to be slowing and, for want of a better word in her head, since she didn't particularly like confined spaces, it seemed to be *struggling* in its descent. She wished it would pick up speed and get her out of the awkward situation. Deep down inside, she knew her response had been overly dramatic and cutting but she was still proud she had found the strength to do it. There were only another fifteen floors and she hoped the elevator would reach the ground before he handed her a business card and she discovered the reason he'd struck up the conversation. Insurance, investment or even real estate. There had to be something behind the smile. Since she was so heavily pregnant, she felt very confident it was not going to segue into a pick-up line.

With her chin lifted slightly, she felt the colour rising in her cheeks; she played with her small pearl earrings the way she always did when she was nervous.

Patrick considered her in silence for a moment as he watched her fidget with the small pearl studs. He had made an uncharacteristic effort to acknowledge her pregnancy and he was taken back at her disparaging remark. He hadn't expected it as she had appeared at first glance to be very sweet. Her pretty face was framed with dark curls and he thought she had an innocence about her. He hadn't foreseen her reaction and to his mind he definitely did not deserve the harsh retort. He wasn't going to take it on the chin.

Without making eye contact as he stared at the same gunmetal door, he decided to answer her abrupt reply with one equally insensitive. 'I think you're the rude one here. You enter a lift, or should I say elevator, due to our location, with only one other person, that being me, and begin a conversation with your unborn children, for which I did not judge you to be mad, but in fact complimented you, and then you remark that I'm rude for making a comment.'

Claudia was surprised by his formal and acerbic rebuttal. His response had been articulate and he had not raised his voice but she wasn't in the mood to eat humble pie. Men, or rather one man, had just let her down very badly and she wasn't going to break her promise to herself. They were all the same if they were given the opportunity. And she had no intention of ever giving a man such an opportunity with her again.

With her eyes facing straight ahead at their shared focal point, she was about to reply when she was stopped by a twinge in her stomach. Her body stiffened with the pain and she hunched a little, almost protectively.

She knew it couldn't be a contraction. It was too early. One hand instinctively reached for her babies and her stomach suddenly felt hard to her touch. She was grateful the stranger was looking away as she leant a little on the elevator wall. She told herself it must be the Braxton Hicks contractions that her obstetrician had mentioned but it seemed to be quite intense and more than a little painful.

It passed quite quickly and finally, after catching her breath, she replied, 'I think it was obvious I was having a private conversation. And clearly you *are* judging me, by implying that I'm mad. That's hardly a nice thing to say to someone you don't know.'

'You're right,' he responded and turned to face her. 'I concede it was less than polite but you have to agree that you most definitely left your manners back up on the thirty-fourth floor.' He looked away as he finished his tersely delivered response and checked for mobile phone reception.

By his abrupt tone and the fact he had noticed which floor she lived on, Claudia looked out of the corner of her eyes at him and wondered for a moment if he was a lawyer. Lawyers always paid attention to details that the general public ignored. Of course, she thought, she would have the slowest ride to the ground with an overbearing man with a legal background. She dropped her chin a little but not to admire her middle; instead she looked tentatively across the elevator to where the man stood. He was wearing highly polished shoes. Slightly raising her chin, she noted his perfectly pressed charcoal-grey slacks and finally, with her head turned a little more in his direction as she gave in to her curiosity, she saw his crisp white shirt and jacket. She had thought initially that he was wearing a suit but on closer, but not too obvious, inspection, she could see flecked threads in the weave. And then there was his expensive Swiss watch. Not forgetting the fact he was already in the elevator when she'd entered, which meant he either lived, or had a client, on the only floor above her. The penthouse on the thirty-fifth floor.

Suddenly she felt another twinge. She wanted to get out of the lift and get to her obstetric appointment immediately. She didn't want to be dragged into a conversation.

'I apologise—I'm sorry,' she returned sharply and without emotion as she once again faced the elevator doors. She rubbed the hollow of her back that was beginning to ache. The niggling pain was spreading and becoming increasingly uncomfortable. She just wanted the short time in the relatively tiny space to be uneventful, so she took the easy option and hoped the conversation would end there.

But it didn't.

'Frankly, I think I'm a little past caring for your less than genuine apology.'

'I beg your pardon?' Claudia knew the handsome stranger had called the situation correctly; she just didn't want to admit it.

'I think you're just giving me lip service,' he continued. 'Forget I said anything nice at all. To be honest, I'm sorry I did, so let's just go back to an awkward silence that comes with sharing an elevator with a stranger and hope the thing picks up speed for both of our sakes.'

Claudia felt a little tug at her heart. The

stranger really had been trying to make pleasant conversation and compliment her in the process and she had shot him down.

'Gosh, I did sound awfully rude, didn't I?' she asked, as much to herself as him. Wishing she had not been as dismissive and had put some meaning behind the words, she offered a more contrite apology. 'I really am sorry. I do mean it.'

'Perhaps.'

Her eyes met his and she could see they were not warm and forgiving but neither were they icy. They were sad. They were filled with a look close to disappointment and she felt her heart sink a little further. She had never been quite so rude to a stranger before. Heaven knew what day he had endured and she had behaved abominably.

Circumstance had made her distrust the male population. She had not even thought how her behaviour would affect the handsome stranger sharing the slowest elevator on the west coast of North America, until he'd pointed it out. But she was surprised by his reaction. She assumed most men would have shrugged it off but he seemed genuinely disappointed, almost as if he was directing the disappointment inward for some reason.

With a humble and heartfelt expression she replied, 'I really do apologise. I'm very sorry and there's really no excuse for my behaviour.' Taking a deep breath, she outstretched her hand like an olive branch. 'I'm Claudia Monticello, slightly hormonal mother-to-be and having a very bad day. I could add that I'm perhaps a little stressed right now as I'm flying back to the UK tomorrow and I have so much still to do. I have to see my obstetrician and finish packing. There's so many things I have to remember…' And so much she wanted to forget. But she had no intention of telling the handsome stranger that.

'Well, perhaps you do have a reason to be a little on edge,' he said, looking into her eyes, almost piercing her soul. 'Apology accepted. Patrick Spencer, doctor, not eavesdropper.'

Claudia smiled. She had picked the wrong profession too. As she kept staring into his eyes, she noticed they were a deep blue with flecks of grey. Like storm clouds swirling over the deepest part of the ocean. She felt herself wondering why he hid such stunning eyes behind dark sunglasses. They were too captivating a shade to be hidden. She shook herself. His eye colour was not something she needed to busy her mind with at that time.

Nothing about him was her concern, she told herself as she noticed there was only a short trip of eight floors until they reached street level and she would never see the man again.

But it did feel strangely reassuring to be in the elevator with a man with a medical background after the fleeting contraction she'd experienced. She knew they were commonplace nearing the latter part of pregnancy and it appeared to have been a once-off but his nearness made her feel a little safer.

No, *very* safe and she didn't know why.

Out of a sense of awkwardness in the silence that were now sharing, she glanced up again to check how many floors they had travelled. The elevator had not picked up any speed. She was glad they weren't in the Burj Khalifa in Dubai or the boys would be ready for pre-school at the rate they were travelling.

With her mind brought to travel, Claudia was excited to be heading home. Once her obstetrician signed her flight clearance she would be on her way back to London. Her contract with the television studio had finally ended, leaving her free to return home. Instinctively, she patted the recent ultrasound scans tucked safely in her bag. She had no swelling in her legs and her blood pressure had been fine at the last visit. Her pregnancy had been uneventful until the twinge, something which was at complete odds with her disastrous personal life. But she was grateful she had something positive upon which to focus.

As they passed the fourth floor and the elevator seemed to almost pause, suddenly she felt another more intense contraction. Claudia tried to smile through it but suspected it was closer to a grimace. Braxton Hicks contractions were a lot different to what she had expected. She had been told that a woman could experience up to four in an hour but she hadn't thought they would be so close together.

Patrick eyed her with concern but, just as he opened his mouth, the stalling elevator came to a jarring halt. Claudia grabbed the railing to steady herself and they both looked up to see the floor light flickering and waited for the doors to open. But they didn't. Instead the lift dropped what she imagined to be another floor and stopped. Patrick had already taken two purposeful steps towards Claudia and she felt his strong arms wrap around her to prevent her from falling. His touch should have worried her but instead a wave of relief washed over her. She was not alone.

'Let's get you on the floor. It will be safer.' Hastily he pulled off his jacket and dropped it to the elevator floor before gently lowering Claudia onto it.

'Your jacket—it will be ruined.'

'At this moment, a ruined jacket is not my concern. You are,' he said matter-of-factly but with an unmistakable warmth in his voice and one Claudia didn't believe she truly deserved after her behaviour. 'When are the babies due?'

'The twins aren't due for another six and a half weeks and I'm fine, really I am,' she insisted as she tried to sit gently and not move and crease the jacket underneath her. 'I'm flying out tomorrow with the doctor's approval; it's the last possible day that the airline will allow me to travel.'

'You're cutting it fine with the whole long haul at almost thirty-four weeks,' he replied with his brows knitted. He added, 'You seemed to be in pain a moment ago.' It was a question he framed as a statement. He didn't want to appear overbearing but he was concerned. He was also doubtful whether she should be travelling at such a late stage of pregnancy. Even with a clean bill of health, it seemed risky for her to take a long haul flight so close to delivering.

'Yes, just one of these Braxton Hicks contractions.'

'You're sure?' His frown had not lifted as he spoke.

This time it was a question and she sensed genuine concern. It heightened hers.

'Absolutely,' she said, followed by a nod. It wasn't the truth. The truth was that she had never been quite so scared in her life but she had to push that reality from her mind and remain positive. The worst-case scenario was too overwhelmingly frightening to consider without collapsing into a heap. She had been holding everything together tenuously for so many months her nerves were threadbare.

'If you say so,' he told her, doubt about her response evident in his tone. 'Just stay seated till we reach the ground.' He retrieved his mobile phone from his trouser pocket, but Claudia assumed there was no reception through the heavy elevator walls as he turned and reached for the emergency telephone.

He didn't take his eyes away from Claudia, even when the standard response finished and he cut in. 'This is Dr Patrick Spencer, I'm in

Terrace Park Towers, Wilshire Boulevard, not far from Highland. We're somewhere between the fourth floor and street level and the elevator's come to a halt. I have a female resident with me. Approximately thirty-four weeks pregnant.' He paused. 'No, no, there's no immediate medical emergency. I have the resident seated and there's no obvious physical injuries but I want a crew to get us out stat. And after the jolt it would be wise to send an ambulance. The patient may need to head to the hospital for a routine obstetric examination.'

With that he hung up and turned his full attention back to Claudia.

Her resolve to remain calm had deserted her, despite attempts to tell herself she was overreacting. She wasn't overreacting. Her eyes darted to the steel doors, willing them to open, and then back to Patrick, unsure what she was willing him to do.

'We'll be out of here before you know it,' he said and very gently wiped the wisps of hair from her brow, now covered in tiny beads of perspiration. 'They're on their way.'

'Yes, they are… I'm afraid.'

'There's nothing to fear. Just stay calm and the crew will have us out of here very quickly.

And there'll be an ambulance on hand if we need one.'

'It's not the crew I'm talking about…it's the babies. I'm afraid my twins are on their way… This isn't Braxton Hicks, Patrick. I'm in labour.'

CHAPTER TWO

CLAUDIA'S WATER BROKE only moments later,
confirming she was very much in labour and
going to deliver her babies in an elevator unless a miracle happened. As she wriggled un-
comfortably on the hard elevator floor with
only Patrick's now soaking wet jacket beneath
her, she stared at nowhere in particular and
prayed with all of her might that it was a bad
dream. One from which she would wake to
find herself giving birth in a pretty delivery
room in a London hospital surrounded by
smiling nurses…nurses just like her sister,
Harriet. She always allayed Claudia's medical concerns with sensible and thoughtful answers delivered in a calm manner, just like
the way their mother had always spoken to
them.

How she wished more than anything that
Harriet was with her. She would know what

to do. She always did…but, as Claudia looked at her surroundings from her new vantage point on the floor, she knew it was pointless to wish for her sister to be there. Or for a birthing suite. She would have neither. Harriet was in Argentina to do something selfless and wonderful and she was paying for her own irresponsible behaviour by being trapped in a Los Angeles elevator in the first stage of labour.

Giving birth to the babies of a man who didn't give a damn.

With the help of another she didn't know.

The next painful wave of contractions broke through her thoughts. Labour had not come on slowly or gently. And there was no point worrying about dust soiling Patrick's jacket; the piece of clothing was now past being saved.

The jacket was of no concern to Patrick, who was kneeling beside Claudia. At that moment he would give a dozen of his finest jackets to make this woman he barely knew comfortable if only he could. But he had nothing close to a dozen of anything to make what lay ahead easier. The situation was dire. There was no way around that fact but Patrick intended to do everything to ensure

Claudia remained calm and focused. All the while he fought his own battle with a past that was rushing back at him. Fine perspiration began lining his brow but he had to push through. He heard Claudia's heavy breathing turn to panting and knew he couldn't give in to his thoughts. Not for even a minute. He had to stay with Claudia.

For the time being at least.

'There's no cell reception but if I can get through on the elevator phone, who can I call? Your husband, boyfriend...your family?'

Claudia shook her head, a little embarrassed by the answer even before she delivered it. Harriet was on and off the communication grid for almost two days while she travelled and even if she could contact her it would be unfair to worry her. And she knew there was no point reaching out to the babies' father. He wouldn't care.

'No, there's no one to call.'

Patrick's eyes met hers in silence. He was surprised and saddened to hear her answer. While she clearly had her defences up initially, Patrick had not suspected for even a moment that a woman like Claudia would be alone in the world.

Unexpectedly, he felt himself being pulled

towards her. He was never pulled towards anyone. Not any more. Not for years. He had locked away the need to feel anything. To need anyone...or to be needed. But suddenly a tenuous and unforeseen bond was forming. And he suspected it was not due just to the confines of the elevator.

Claudia wriggled some more and looked down at the jacket. 'I'm so sorry...'

'Claudia—' he cut in as he looked intently into her eyes, not shifting his gaze for even a moment, not allowing himself to betray, to any degree, the very real risks that he knew lay ahead '—you're in labour and you think I'm worried about a jacket.'

'But it's ruined.'

'The only thing I care about now is finding something clean for the babies. Do you have anything in your bag? Anything I can wrap them in?'

Claudia shook her head. While her bag was the fashionably oversized style, it held very little, other than her wallet, apartment keys, her phone, a thin, flimsy scarf, a small cosmetic purse and a bottle of water. And her ultrasound films.

Patrick couldn't wait any longer. There would be two babies arriving and they needed to have something clean to rest upon while he tended to their mother. He was not going to put them on the floor of the elevator. Without hesitating, he began to unbutton his white linen shirt and, slipping it from his very toned and lightly tanned body, he spread it out.

Claudia knew she was staring. She was helpless to pull her gaze away. The man about to deliver her babies had stripped bare to the waist. It was overwhelming and almost too much for her to process. The whole situation was quickly morphing from a bad dream into a nightmare. She was about to give birth to the sons of a man who didn't love her and they would be delivered by a half-naked stranger in a broken elevator. Tears began welling in her eyes as the waves of another contraction came. This one was more powerful than the last and she struggled to hide the level of pain.

Patrick reached for her hand. 'I want you to squeeze my hand when the contractions happen.'

'I'll be fine,' she told him as the contraction passed and she felt uncomfortable getting any closer to the semi-naked stranger than she already was. His arms looked lean but powerful. And she could smell the light tones of his musky cologne.

'I know you'll be fine but if you squeeze my hand each time you have a contraction I'll know how close together they are.'

'I think you will be able to tell without me squeezing your hand.'

Patrick nodded. 'Have it your way, but my hand is here if you need it.'

Still feeling wary, Claudia eyed him suspiciously, wondering who this man was, this man who was so willing to come to her aid. Only a few minutes before, they had exchanged less than friendly words. Now the man she had initially assumed to be a lawyer hiding a hangover behind dark glasses was in fact a doctor literally on bended knees helping her.

'The contractions seem to be evenly spaced at the moment,' he said, breaking through her thoughts.

'But they're awfully close and awfully painful. Does that mean the babies will be here soon?'

'It could but it's impossible to tell.' Patrick hoped that it would be a prolonged labour. Prolonged enough to allow the technical team to open the elevator doors and bring in help.

'Do you think there's any chance they will get us out before my babies arrive?'

'They're doing their best.'

Ten minutes passed with no news from outside and two more contractions. Claudia caught her breath and leant back against the cold walls of the elevator. It was soothing on her now clammy skin. The air was starting to warm up, and she imagined it would be stifling in a short time if the doors were not opened soon. But they would be. She had to hold on to the belief that any minute paramedics would burst through the steel barriers and transport her to hospital.

Patrick stretched his long legs out in front of him and rested against the adjacent cool wall. 'So which London hospital had you planned on having the boys?' he asked as he looked up at the ceiling for no particular reason. All sense of reason had left the elevator when Claudia began labour.

'I thought the Wright Street Women's and Children's Hospital. I checked in online a few months back and it has a lovely birthing centre with floral wallpaper and midwives and everything my babies and I would need. I've booked an appointment with a midwife there next week.'

'Well, you won't be needing that appointment. Not for this delivery anyway, but perhaps you could book in for your next baby.'

'I'm not sure there will be a next,' she replied quickly with raised eyebrows, still not forgetting the pain of the contraction that had barely passed.

'Perhaps you will change your mind and have more but these children will definitely be born in LA. With any luck, the paramedics will have us out soon and they'll be born at the Mercy Hospital.'

Claudia felt her pulse race a little. 'What if that doesn't happen?'

Patrick turned to her and took her hand in his. Suddenly the sensation of her warm skin on his made him feel something more than he had felt in many years. It made him feel close to being alive. He swallowed and pushed away the feeling. That sort of intimacy had no place in his life. For the last decade, whenever he felt a woman's body against his, there was nothing more than mutual pleasure. It didn't mean anything to either of them. They served a purpose to each other and walked away. Feeling anything more was not worth the risk.

He couldn't get attached to a woman he didn't know who was about to give birth to the children of another man. The idea was ridiculous.

'Let's not go there, Claudia. The medical team will be here soon.'

'But they may not...' she argued.

'Then we'll bring two healthy boys into the world on our own.' He said it instinctively but as the words escaped his mouth he prayed it would not come to that.

Claudia took another deep breath. There was a chance they weren't going to be rescued. And she had to prepare herself for the imminent wave of the next contraction and then worse. She closed her eyes.

Patrick studied her. 'Now don't go closing your beautiful eyes on me,' he told her. 'I need you to listen to me and work with me. You will get through this but you have to stay strong. You have your children to think of.'

Slowly she forced her lids open and found herself looking into the warmest eyes she had ever seen. Her stomach did a little somersault and it wasn't a contraction.

'That's better,' he told her with a smile

filled with so much warmth she thought her heart would melt. Everything he was making her feel was unexpected. And the feelings seemed so real. Was it just the intense situation they were facing or was there something about the man that was very different from anyone she had ever met?

She wasn't sure.

But his nearness was affecting her. She doubted he was trying to affect—he just was.

'What about you—do you have any children? Did your family move here to LA too?' She rattled off successive questions, trying to deflect the blush she suddenly feared he had brought to her cheeks. She could see there was no wedding band on his hand but, as she knew first-hand, the lack of a ring on a man's finger did not bring any certainty there was no wife. It was out of character for her to be so direct but nothing about the situation was normal.

'No, I'm not married, Claudia, and the rest of my family...well, they're back in the UK...' Patrick's words trailed off. He wasn't about to tell Claudia about his life, his past or his loss. After twelve years it was still raw at times but now focusing on Claudia removed his desire to give any consideration to his own pain. He had to be in the moment for the woman who needed him. He couldn't think about what had happened all those years ago or the price he still paid every day.

He had to let something go.

And that had to be the past—for the time being. But he knew that it would come back to him. It always did.

'Do you want children one day? I guess if you've done this before, bringing them into the world would make you want a brood or run the other way,' she cut in again. As she felt the warmth in her face subside she was slightly relieved on that front but the need for the banter continued. Any distraction would do.

He felt a muscle in his jaw twitch. She was unwittingly making it very hard to stay in the moment. 'No,' he said, not wanting to go into any detail. The answer was not that he didn't like children; in fact it ran far deeper than that. Children meant family and he never planned on being part of a family again. The pain still lingered, twelve years after he had been forced to walk away from his own.

'So am I right—you don't want to take your job home?'

'You're full of questions, aren't you?'

Claudia didn't answer. She felt the next contraction building and as it rolled in she couldn't say anything. She dropped her head to her chest and took in shallow breaths.

Without prompting, Patrick's hands gently massaged her back. Instinctively, he knew what was happening and he kept up the physical therapy until it passed. And then a few moments longer.

She felt his hands linger, then shook herself back to reality. He was a doctor doing his job. Nothing more.

'Why did you move to LA?' she piped up, then bit her lip as she realised it was none of her business and she had no clue what had driven her to ask him such personal questions. She felt as if the pain had taken over her mind. She was acting like a different person, someone who suddenly wanted to know everything about Patrick. Perhaps it was to distract herself. Perhaps not. But she knew the moment the words fell from her mouth that she had overstepped the boundaries of polite conversation. 'Please forget I asked. Blame it on the stress. I really am exhibiting the worst manners today. I've asked the most improper questions and ruined your jacket...'

'Forgiven for both.' Patrick hesitated. 'I

guess I'm just a private person, Claudia. I'm happy to answer any medical questions, anything at all, but I'd prefer to leave the rest alone. Suffice to say, my family and I didn't see eye to eye about something that happened and this opportunity came up. So I left London and headed here.'

'Oh, I'm sorry.' Claudia suddenly felt even more embarrassed that she had asked but she also felt a little sad for him. She barely knew the man but, with the way he was taking care of her, she suddenly felt that she wanted to be on *his side* in a situation she knew nothing about.

Patrick knew it sounded as if they had parted ways on something insignificant. He thought it was best to leave it at that. There was no need to mention that he'd made the opportunity to allow him to move to the US. It was something he'd had to do to help everyone with their grief. To not be there, reminding them every day of what had happened.

It was not the time or place to tell a woman he had just met that his sister had died.

And he had taken the blame for her death.

An unspoken agreement not to revisit the conversation about his family was made in the awkward silence by both of them.

'I'll need to examine you in a few minutes and assess whether you have begun to dilate and, if you have, if the first baby is visible,' he told her as he pulled himself from the past back to where he belonged.

Suddenly the elevator lights began to flicker. Claudia bit her lip nervously. She felt her chin begin to quiver but was powerless to stop it. All questions disappeared. She didn't want anything from Patrick other than reassurance that her babies would survive.

Patrick drew a deep breath but managed to keep his body language in check. If they lost the lights, then he could not convince himself there would be a good outcome but he would never let Claudia know that. He even refused to admit it to himself.

'I need to do the exam while we still have some lights to work with; if we lose them it will be challenging as I'll have to work by feel alone. But, whatever happens, I'm here for you and your babies, Claudia, and together we'll all get throughout this,' Patrick told her with a firmness and urgency that did not disguise the seriousness of the situation, but he also managed to make her feel secure in the knowledge that he was with her all the way. He filled his lungs with the warm air that surrounded them, determined he would do his damnedest to make his prayers a reality.

She nodded her consent as the contraction began to subside, along with her uncontrollable need to push.

'Breathe slowly and deeply,' he said while he stroked her arm and waited for the contraction to pass before he began his examination. Twins made the birth so much more complicated, along with his lack of equipment and the risk of losing the lights.

'Have you delivered many babies?'

'Yes, I've delivered many babies, Claudia, but never in an elevator and not for...'

The elevator phone rang and stopped Patrick from explaining how long it had been since his last delivery. Instinctively, he answered the phone. 'Yes?'

'This is the utilities manager. We're working to have you out as soon as possible but it may be another twenty minutes to half an hour. Our only rostered technician is across town. How's the young woman?'

'She's in labour.'

'Hell... Okay, that's gonna be brutal on her.' The man's knee-jerk reaction was loud. 'I'll put the tech to get here ASAP or get an off-duty one over there stat. We've already got an ambulance en route.'

'That would be advisable,' Patrick responded in an even tone, not wanting to add to Claudia's building distress. 'I'm about to assess her progress but you need to ensure there are two ambulances waiting when your technician gets us out. We're dealing with the birth of two premature infants so ensure the paramedics are despatched with humidicribs and you have an obstetrician standing by with a birthing kit including cord clamps and Syntocinon.' Then he lowered his voice and added, 'And instruct them to bring plasma. There's always the slight risk of a postpartum haemorrhage.' With that he hung up the phone to let the team outside do their best to get medical help to them as soon as possible.

He immediately turned his attention back to Claudia, who lay against the elevator wall with small beads of perspiration building on her brow and the very palpable fear of what lay ahead written on her face.

'I don't want my babies to die.'

'Claudia, you need to listen to me,' he began with gentleness in his voice along with a reassuring firmness. 'We *are* going to get through this. Your babies will be fine but you need to help me.'

Claudia couldn't look at him. She couldn't lift her gaze from her stomach and the babies inside of her. Fear surged through her veins. It was real. They weren't getting out of the elevator. No one was coming to rescue them. No one was going to take her to the hospital. The harsh reality hit her. Her babies would be born inside the metal walls that surrounded them.

And they might not survive.

'I am going to have to cut your underwear free. I don't want to try and lift you and remove it.'

Claudia felt her heart race and her mind spin. She was losing control and the fear was not just physical. Deep inside, she knew the odds were stacked against her and her boys but she appreciated that Patrick hadn't voiced that. The man with the sunglasses wasn't anything close to what she'd thought. He was about to bring her sons into the world.

And she suddenly had no choice but to trust him.

Her hand ran across her mouth and tugged at her lips nervously. 'Fine, just do it,' she managed to say as she steeled herself for what was about to happen to her, her boys and Patrick as the urge to push and the pain began to overtake her senses once again.

Patrick ripped off the gloves that had handled the elevator telephone, covered his hands in antibacterial solution and slipped on another pair of gloves. Carefully using sterile scissors, he gently cut her underwear from her and checked the progress of her labour.

'You are fully dilated and your first son's head is visible,' he told her. 'Labour is moving fast and you're doing great. Just keeping breathing slowly…'

His words were cut short by the cry she gave with the next painful contraction. More painful than the previous one.

'I can't do this. I can't.'

'Yes, you can.'

'Should I be as scared to death as I am right now?'

'No,' he said, leaning in towards her. 'Just remember, Claudia, you're not alone. We'll get through this together. You and I will bring your babies into the world.'

He prayed, as every word slipped from his now dry mouth, that he could do what he promised. He had the expertise, he reminded himself. But he also knew that was not always enough. There were some situations that no skills could fight.

Steeling himself, he knew he was prepared to fight for Claudia and her boys.

She closed her eyes and swallowed.

'I need you to try and get onto your hands and knees…'

'Why?' Her eyes opened wide. 'I thought you have babies lying on your back. Is there something wrong?' Panic showed on her face as she stared into Patrick's eyes, searching for reassurance but frightened of what he might tell her.

'It will be easier on you and your babies if you're on all fours,' he told her. 'It opens up the birth canal and, even though it may seem uncomfortable, believe me, it will be far better than being on your back. Just try it. Here, I'll help you.'

He reached for her and she felt the warmth and strength in his hold as his hands guided her into the position he needed to best deliver the babies. He made sure her hands and knees were still resting on the damp jacket, not the bare floor.

'I'd like to put a cool compress on you. It's getting warm in here but I'm running out of clothing to give you.'

Even in pain, Claudia smiled at his remark. It was true. He had given his jacket and his shirt. 'There's a clean scarf in my bag but it's very small. You could wet that.'

Patrick reached for her large tan leather bag and dragged it unceremoniously across the metal flooring. He emptied the contents onto the floor, found the small patterned scarf and then noticed the films.

'Are those films for your obstetrician?'

She turned her head slightly. 'Yes, he was going to check them and then sign the papers to allow me to fly home to London.'

He pushed the envelope to the side and took her bottle of water and sparingly dampened the scarf. Gently lifting the sweat-dampened curls on the nape of her neck, he rested the tiny compress on her hot skin. There was nothing he could do about whatever showed on the films now. They wouldn't change anything in the confines of the elevator. He had no idea what the next few minutes would hold but he would be beside her and do whatever he could to keep Claudia and her babies alive.

Feeling his hand on her skin felt so calming and reassuring and Claudia wondered if it was the touch of his skin against hers as much as the makeshift compress. But neither gave relief when the next powerful contraction came and she cried out with the pain.

Her cries tugged at Patrick's heart. He hated the fact there was nothing he could do. But he needed to focus on delivering both babies or risk losing them all. He wouldn't let that happen.

Suddenly the first baby began to enter the world. A mass of thick black hair curled like a halo around his perfect tiny face.

'Just push slowly and think about your breathing,' he instructed her. 'We need that to control the baby's arrival. We don't want to rush him. You can tear your skin and I want to avoid that.'

The urge to give a giant push was overwhelming but Claudia knew she had to let her breathing slow the pace. She thought of Patrick's handsome face and tried to follow his instructions. There were a few more contractions and finally Claudia's first baby was born into Patrick's waiting hands. He let out a tiny cry as Patrick quickly cleared his mouth of mucous and quickly checked his vital signs.

The baby was small but not so small as to put him in immediate danger by not having access to a humidicrib. Patrick had feared he might have been tinier considering the gestational age and the fact he was a twin. He clamped the cord with a sterile surgical tie before he laid him on the shirt. The baby had endured a harsh entry into the world and the shirt was a far cry from a soft landing but, until his brother was born, there was little Patrick could do for the new arrival. He could not put the child to Claudia's breast as she needed to remain on all fours until the second baby was delivered.

Another contraction began and the second baby was quickly on its way. Patrick hoped that he would not be faced with a foot. That would mean a breech birth and complications he did not want to contemplate.

That next painful contraction came and Claudia cried out loudly but managed with each following breath to push her second baby head first into the world. And once again into Patrick's arms, where the baby took his first breath and cried for the first time. Patrick checked the second baby's vital signs and again was relieved that the delivery had no complications. It had progressed far better than Patrick had imagined.

With beads of perspiration now covering her entire body, Claudia looked over at her two sons and felt a love greater than she'd thought possible.

And a closeness to the man who had delivered them. He was like her knight in shining armour. And she would be indebted to him forever.

Quite apart from being an amazing doctor, Patrick was a wonderful man.

Through the fog of her emotionally drained state, Claudia suddenly suspected her feelings for Patrick ran deeper than simply gratitude for saving them all.

Patrick remained quiet. There were still two afterbirths and Claudia to consider. Despite the peaceful and contented look she wore, he knew they were not out of the woods yet.

Gently he placed the second baby next to his tiny brother and wrapped the shirt around them both before he carefully helped Claudia from her knees onto her back again. He grabbed her leather bag and made a makeshift pillow for her head. Claudia was past caring about the bag or her own comfort as she watched her tiny sons lying so close to her.

Patrick reached for them. 'I'm going to rest the babies on you while we wait for the afterbirth.'

While the delivery had been relatively straightforward, Patrick was aware that Claudia's double birth put her at increased risk of haemorrhage. Gently he placed the two tiny boys into their mother's arms and he watched as her beautiful face lit up further as she cradled them. Her beauty seemed to be magnified with the boys now securely with her and, with her genes, they would no doubt be very handsome young men.

Within minutes, part of the placenta was delivered but as Patrick examined it he was concerned that it was not intact. Claudia would require a curette in hospital if the remaining placenta wasn't expelled. But, that aside and despite the surroundings, Claudia had delivered two seemingly healthy boys. Patrick took a deep breath and filled his lungs as he looked at Claudia with a sense of pride for the strength shown by a woman he barely knew.

Then he noticed her face had become a little pale.

'I sort of feel a little cold now,' she said softly, as her body began to shiver. 'It feels odd; I was so hot before. There's no pain but...'

Patrick noticed her eyes were becoming

glassy and she was losing her grip on the boys. There was something very wrong. Quickly he scooped them from her weakening hold and placed them together beside her, still wrapped in his shirt. He felt for her pulse. It was becoming fainter. He looked down to see blood pouring from Claudia and pooling on the jacket underneath her.

It was his worst nightmare—a postpartum haemorrhage.

Claudia had fifty percent more blood in her body because of the pregnancy, which would help, but, with the amount of blood she had already lost on the floor, it would still only buy them a small amount of time. He needed to encourage her uterus to contract, shutting off the open blood vessels. Immediately he began to massage her belly through to her uterus but after a minute he could see there was no difference. She was barely lucid and he needed to administer a synthetic form of the hormone that would naturally assist, but that was on the other side of the closed elevator doors with the paramedics. It wasn't something he carried in his medical bag. Not now anyway. Once he would have had everything he now needed to save Claudia—but that was a lifetime ago.

'Claudia—' he ceased the massage momentarily and patted her hand '—I need you to try to feed one of the boys. It will help to stimulate a hormone that will lessen the bleeding. Do you understand?'

'Uh-huh,' she muttered while trying to keep her eyes from closing. 'I feel so light-headed.'

'That's the blood loss. I'm going to do everything I can to stop it until help arrives, but again we need to work together. You'll be on your way to hospital very soon.'

He reached down and gently unwrapped the babies and, picking up the larger of the twins, he lifted Claudia's tank top and bra and placed him onto her breast. Instinctively the baby latched onto his mother and began to suckle while Patrick continued the massaging.

'Do you have any names for the boys?' he asked, trying to keep Claudia focused as he dealt with the medical emergency that was unfolding before his eyes.

She tried to think but the names weren't there. They were special names and they should have spilled out without any effort but she was befuddled, which wasn't her. 'I think…' She paused momentarily as the names she had chosen now seemed strangely out of reach. She blinked to bring herself back on track. 'Thomas…and Luca…after each of their great-grandpas.'

'I think they are strong names for two little fighters. Is this baby Thomas or Luca?'

Claudia smiled down at her son, still attached to her breast but not really sucking successfully. 'Thomas…but I think he's tired already and a bit too small.'

'I think you're right on both counts.'

'I'm feeling quite dizzy again.' She paused as she felt herself wavering and her vision was starting to blur. Fear was mounting again inside her. 'Am I going to die?'

'No, you're going to pull through and raise your two sons until they are grown men.'

Claudia felt weaker by the minute. She knew there was something very serious happening, even though she couldn't see the blood. 'If I don't make it…'

'You will,' he argued as he reached for Thomas, who was unable to suckle, and placed him safely on the floor beside his brother, Luca.

She closed her eyes for a moment. She felt too weak to fight. 'You need to contact my sister, Harriet. Her details are in my phone. She needs to be there for my boys if I can't be.'

'Claudia, listen to me. You're going to make it, but I'm going to have to do something very uncomfortable for you.'

'What?' she asked in a worried whisper.

'I'm going to compress your uterus with my hands. It will further slow the bleeding.'

She nodded but she felt as if she was close to drifting off to sleep. 'If you have to, then do it.'

'Try to stay awake,' he pleaded with her as he attempted to manually compress the uterus with the firm pressure of his hands.

Minutes passed but still the blood was flowing over his hands to the floor beneath her. Claudia needed to be in a hospital and she needed to be there now. This was something more serious than the usual postpartum blood loss.

She was dangerously close to losing consciousness as he gently removed his hands. The manual pressure could not stop the bleeding. Claudia needed surgical intervention if she was to survive. He reached for the films and ripped open the envelope. The films scattered on the floor but, as he grabbed the report, his worst fears were confirmed. Claudia's placenta had invaded the walls of her uterus. Every part of his body shuddered. It was déjà vu. The prognosis was identical to what he had faced all those years ago. There was no way her obstetrician would have allowed her to board a plane with the condition. Claudia would have delivered her sons in America, whether it had been this day or another.

With a heavy heart, he dropped his gloves and the report to the floor and pulled a barely conscious Claudia into his arms, where he held her while he stroked the faces of the little boys lying on the floor beside them. If help didn't arrive within a few minutes he would lose Claudia.

And her two tiny babies would never know their beautiful, brave mother.

CHAPTER THREE

As Claudia's body suddenly fell limp in Patrick's arms, he heard the doors open behind him and instantly felt a firm grip on his bare shoulder.

'We've got it from here,' the deep voice said.

Patrick turned his head to see a full medical team rushing towards them. He had never been happier in his life than he was at that moment and, with adrenaline surging through his veins, he immediately began firing instructions at lightning speed. The miracle Claudia needed had arrived at the moment he had run out of options.

'We're dealing with a postpartum haemorrhage—she needs Syntocinon immediately and a catheter inserted so that the uterus has a better chance of contracting with an empty bladder. If she doesn't stabilise she'll be looking at a transfusion. Forget cross-matching as there may not be time; just start plasma now and have O negative waiting in OR.'

Patrick moved away as the medical team stepped in to begin the treatment he had ordered. Immediately they inserted an IV line, began a plasma transfusion then administered some pain relief and Syntocinon in an attempt to stop Claudia's bleeding while another two paramedics collected the baby boys and left the elevator with them securely inside portable humidicribs.

'Any idea why she's still bleeding?' the attending doctor asked.

'Placenta accreta,' Patrick said as he reached for the films lying on the floor. He kept his voice low so he would not alarm Claudia. 'I checked the report on the ultrasound films. Only a very small amount of the placenta was delivered and the rest is still firmly entrenched in the uterus wall. If the report is correct, she may be looking at a surgery but a complete hysterectomy should be the surgeon's last option. I doubt she's more than late twenties, if that, so she might like to keep her womb.'

'I'm sure they'll proceed conservatively if they can.'

Patrick nodded. He had no idea what the

future would hold for Claudia and he wanted her to have every choice possible. 'The boys appear fine but they'll need a thorough examination with the paediatrician,' Patrick continued, not taking his eyes from Claudia. 'One is a little smaller than the other but let's hope there's no underlying issues with their premature arrival.'

'You did a remarkable job, all things considered,' the paramedics told Patrick as they watched the barely conscious Claudia being lifted onto the gurney and then securely but gently strapped in.

Keeping his attention on Claudia, who was beginning to show signs of being lucid, the doctor added, 'And you, young lady, are very lucky this man was sharing the elevator. It would not have been this outcome without him, that's for certain. You and your boys all owe your lives to him.'

Claudia smiled a meek smile and held out her hand in an effort to show her gratitude. Patrick cupped it gently in his own strong hands and smiled back at her then he turned to the attending doctor. 'I'll be travelling sidesaddle to the hospital if there's room.'

'There's definitely room.'

* * *

For a little over three hours, Patrick divided his time between pacing the corridors outside Recovery and visiting the Neonatal Intensive Care Unit to check on Luca and Thomas. They had given him a consulting coat to cover his bare chest upon arrival at the hospital. Claudia's dark-haired boys, one with sparkling blue eyes and the other with deep brown like their mother, were doing very well and he felt a deep and very unexpected bond with them. A bond that he hadn't felt towards anyone, let alone tiny people, for more years than he cared to remember.

But these boys were special, perhaps because he'd delivered them in a crisis, or perhaps because their mother was clearly a very special woman. Perhaps it was both but, whatever was driving him to stay, he knew the three of them were bringing out protective feelings in him. A sense that he was needed and almost as if he belonged there. He should have felt unnerved and wanted to run but he didn't. That need to protect himself from being hurt was overridden by the need to protect Claudia, Thomas and Luca.

Both boys weighed a little over four pounds, which was a relief. They were still in their humidicribs and being monitored closely but both had passed all the paediatrician's initial tests and were being gavage fed by the neonatal nurses when Patrick left the nursery and headed back to check on their mother. Her surgery had taken far longer than he had anticipated. He had for a moment contemplated scrubbing in to assist when they'd arrived in Emergency and were rushed around to the OR but he'd immediately thought better of it. A reality check reminded him that his last obstetric surgery had ended his career.

Patrick wanted her to be spared the additional stress and long-term repercussions of the hysterectomy if possible and voiced that again upon arrival. The surgical resident had reassured Patrick that Dr Sally Benton was well respected in the field of gynaecological surgery and that Claudia would be in expert hands. Patrick hoped that the option to give birth again one day in the pretty delivery room with floral wallpaper, midwives and pain relief was not taken away. But, three hours later, he knew the reality of her surgery taking so long meant she had probably undergone a hysterectomy. And she would have to give up on that dream.

'I'm Sally Benton.' She pulled her surgical cap free and outstretched her hand.

'Patrick Spencer,' he responded as he met her handshake. He looked at the woman before him. She was tall and thin, her short black hair with smatterings of grey framed her pretty face and he suspected she was in her early fifties.

'Dr Spencer, I assume.'

'Yes.'

'I wanted to personally thank you for the medical intervention you provided in the elevator. Miss Monticello is in Recovery now and she certainly wouldn't be if you hadn't done such an amazing job delivering her sons and keeping her alive. If you hadn't been with her today, there would most definitely have been a question mark over their survival.'

Patrick drew a deep breath and chose to ignore the compliment. 'Was it conservative surgery?'

'No, unfortunately, Miss Monticello underwent a full hysterectomy to stop the haemorrhaging. She retained her ovaries but her uterus has been removed,' Dr Benton continued as she took a seat in the corridor and indicated Patrick to do the same. 'The attending doctor briefed me on your diagnosis of suspected placenta accreta, but the depth of invasion was not first but second grade. I was faced with placenta increta as the chorionic villi had invaded the muscular layer of the uterine wall so I had no option but to remove her womb. She was lucky that it had not spread through the uterine wall to other organs such as the bladder. Let's just say I'm glad I didn't have to deal with that; as you would know, even in this day and age, there's still a six to seven percent mortality rate for that, due to the complications.'

Patrick knew the statistics for death only too well.

'Thank you, Dr Benton.'

'Don't thank me. As I said before, you did the hard work keeping her alive. And she has two wonderful little boys. Perhaps the loss of her womb will not be a complete tragedy.'

Patrick nodded. He wondered how Claudia would react to the need for a hysterectomy.

'And how are her sons doing?' the surgeon enquired.

'Very well,' Patrick said with a sense of pride that surprised him. 'They're handsome young men and a good weight for their gestational age.'

'Great. Now that's out of the way and we've

spoken about our mutual patients, I have a personal question for you,' Dr Benton continued. 'How do you know Miss Monticello?'

'We were just sharing the elevator.'

Her expression revealed her surprise. 'Well, that's serendipity for you. I don't think she could have asked for a better travelling companion. Where do you practice obstetrics?' Then, without waiting for an answer, she added, 'Am I right in assuming, with your accent, and because I haven't heard of you around LA, that your practice is out of state or perhaps abroad?'

Patrick hesitated. He didn't want to talk about himself but he knew the doctor sitting beside him had every right to enquire. 'No, I practice here in LA but I'm not in OBGYN.'

'Really?' Her brow wrinkled as she considered his response. 'What's your field then?'

'I'm a board certified cosmetic surgeon.'

Once again, she didn't hide her surprise. 'I'd never have picked that,' she said with a grin on her somewhat tired face as she stood up and again offered a handshake. 'Well, Dr Spencer, if you ever get tired of your current field, you should consider obstetrics. There's a shortage of experts in the field and you're very skilled. Your intervention was nothing short of amazing in the conditions you were forced to work in. As I said, Miss Monticello owes her life to you. She will be in her room in another two hours or so. She lost a lot of blood, as you know, so we'll be monitoring her in Recovery for a little longer than we normally would. But I'm sure she'd be pleased to see you.'

Patrick met her handshake and she smiled before she left him alone.

Patrick spent the next two hours with Luca and Thomas. He had called his practice and rearranged his schedule. While the boys were being monitored closely he still didn't want to leave. Not yet anyway. Thomas was in a humidicrib and Luca required additional oxygen to be provided through an oxy-hood so he was in an open bed warmer. The neonatologist felt certain that would only be a temporary measure as both appeared to be healthy and a satisfactory weight for their gestational age. Patrick was aware they had some basic milestones to achieve, both in weight and development, before they would be released; he doubted it would be more than three or four weeks before they would be allowed to leave hospital with their mother.

He went downstairs to the florist and picked the largest floral bouquet they had and two brown bears with blue bows. Claudia had told him she had no one she could reach out to and he knew how that felt only too well. He tried not to think of what he had lost when he'd walked away from his family.

Only now at least Claudia did have two little people to call her family. Still, he knew her room would be devoid of anything to brighten her day and lift her spirits and, after the day she had endured, she deserved a room filled with flowers. And something to remind her of the boys when she was resting and not able to be with them in the neonatal nursery. And when she had to face the reality of the hysterectomy she had undergone without her consent.

The nurse at the station arranged for the flowers to be placed near her bed.

Waiting outside the room twenty minutes later, he couldn't contain, nor fully understand, the smile that spread across his face and the warmth that surged through his body when he saw her hospital bed being wheeled down the corridor towards him. She was still pale but not as drained as when he had last seen her, and she hadn't noticed him. In the pit of his stomach he still remembered her limp body collapsing against his and he'd thought the boys had lost their mother.

Patiently he remained outside as she was settled into her room but, as the nurses exited, he tapped on the door that was ajar.

'Are you up to a visitor?'

'Patrick?'

'How did you guess?' he asked as he quietly entered her room. 'Perhaps it's the British accent—there are not a lot of us around these parts so I guess it's a giveaway.'

'In this city, it's a dead giveaway.' It was more than just his accent, but Claudia couldn't tell Patrick that it was also his reassuring tone that told her exactly who was at her door. It was the same strong voice that had kept her going when she'd wanted to give up. It was the voice of the man who had saved her and her sons.

'May I come in?'

'Of course,' she said, ushering him in with the arm that wasn't connected to the IV providing pain relief after her surgery. 'What are you still doing here?'

'Keeping an eye on…your handsome young sons.'

'They are gorgeous, aren't they? The nurses

wheeled me on the bed into the nursery to see them a few minutes ago on the way back from Recovery. They were sleeping but they told me they're both doing very well.' She paused and nervously chewed on the inside of her cheek to keep her emotions under control. 'Thanks to you.'

Patrick moved closer to her in the softly lit room. 'Not because of me; you did the hard work, Claudia. I just assisted.'

'Maybe the hard work, but you did the skilled work. Without you,' she began, then her chin quivered as she struggled again to keep her tears at bay, 'they could have…well, they might not have made it if you weren't there with me.'

He reached for her hand. It was instinctive and something he had not been driven to do in a very long time. 'Not a chance. They're as strong as their mother.'

Claudia looked down at his hand covering hers. After the trauma of the preceding hours, it made her feel secure. But she couldn't get used to that feeling of being safe. Not with anyone, no matter how kind. She knew that she and Patrick were bonded by what they had been through and it was a normal re-action to the traumatic experience they'd shared. But now, in the safety of the hospital, she had to accept it was nothing more. Although he had proven her initial assumption of him very wrong, she couldn't afford to get swept away by some romantic notion there was more to it. As if he'd appeared like her white knight, saved her and would steal her away to his castle. That wasn't the real world.

Knowing she needed to create some distance between them, she slipped her hand free and haphazardly ran her fingers through her messy curls that had been swept up in a surgical cap for hours.

The move was not lost on Patrick and he graciously accepted her subtle rebuff. He had overstepped the mark. And he never overstepped the mark with a woman. Perhaps it was because she looked so lost and vulnerable that he wanted to make her feel less alone, but clearly she was not looking to be saved again. And he needed to step away. He was grateful she'd reminded him subtly that he wasn't looking to become attached to anyone.

That time in his life had passed. Being alone was what he did best. *What had he been thinking?*

'So…how are you feeling?' he asked in a doctor-patient tone. 'Your body has been through a lot today, quite apart from bringing Thomas and Luca into the world.'

'You mean the…hysterectomy?'

He nodded then waited in silence to hear Claudia's response to the emergency life-changing surgery. She was a resilient woman but he knew this would certainly test any woman and he would not be surprised if she struggled to come to terms with it.

She dropped her gaze for a moment then, lifting her chin and her eyes almost in defiance at what the universe had dealt her, she nodded. 'I'll be okay. I'm alive and I have my sons. It would be stupid to mourn what I can't change and perhaps it would be selfish to ask for more than what I was given today. My life and the lives of my children is miracle enough.'

Patrick was already in awe of the strength that she had shown in the elevator but her reaction to the news almost brought him to his knees with respect for her courage and acceptance of what she couldn't change. She was a truly remarkable woman.

Her fingers nervously played with the woven blanket for a minute before she looked back at Patrick. 'When I think of how terribly wrong everything could have gone today, losing my womb is a small price to pay.'

While Claudia looked like a porcelain doll, Patrick had learned over the few hours since their lives collided that she was made of far tougher material. Still, it puzzled him that she was alone in the world. Had she pushed people from it? Or had they abandoned her? Had being alone made her that strong? He couldn't imagine anyone walking away from such an amazing woman.

Then he realised none of his questions mattered. She had been his unofficial patient for a few hours. Nothing more.

'That huge arrangement of flowers is stunning. I'm guessing it's from you,' she added as she looked around the room and spied the huge bouquet on a shelf near her. It was getting dark outside and she could see the lights of the Los Angeles skyline. But the flowers were more spectacular than any view.

Patrick nodded and tried to look at her with the doctor-patient filter but it was becoming a struggle with each passing moment. It had been an intense first meeting in the elevator but there was more pulling him to her than the fact he had delivered her babies under such conditions. They were not in the confines of that small space any more and she no longer needed his help but still he wanted to be there for the stunning brunette still dressed in a shapeless white surgical gown.

And he was confused as hell. He had unexpectedly become a passenger on a roller coaster of his own emotions. Before, he had always been the driver. He needed to gain control. Quickly. He needed to make it less personal.

'Have you noticed how drab the walls in these rooms are? I needed to brighten your room somehow. I thought flowers would do the trick.'

'The rooms are not that bad, young man,' a stern voice replied from the doorway. 'My name's Vanda, and it would do you well not to complain. I'll be tending to your wife tonight and, for your interest...'

'Oh...we're not married,' came their reply in unison.

There was a moment's uncomfortable silence as the three of them looked at each other in silence.

'Sorry if I presumed your marital status; it's just habit at my age,' the nurse, who Patrick imagined to be in her early fifties, with short auburn hair and twinkling blue eyes, said. She crossed the room, manoeuvring around Patrick to get access to her patient. 'I have two grandchildren and their parents aren't married either. *Haven't got time*, they say. Well, as long as they're happy, I'm happy.'

'No, we're not together,' Claudia began before the nurse wrapped the blood pressure monitor around her arm. 'He's my...' She paused, not knowing how to describe Patrick. *What was their relationship?* she wondered. They weren't friends, but nor were they connected as patient and doctor in a formal sense. Their relationship really couldn't be defined...not easily at least...except, perhaps, for *intense* and *sudden*.

'I'm her emergency elevator obstetrician... not the father of her babies.'

As Patrick said the words, he wondered, against his better judgement, who was the father of her children. What sort of man was he? And why wasn't he rushing to Claudia's side? Patrick knew that if he was the father, no matter how forcefully the mother of his children tried to push him away, he would stand fast to the spot.

But he wasn't the father of Claudia's children or anyone's children. And he never would be.

'Oh, of course, you're the young woman who delivered in the elevator this afternoon,' Vanda answered. She confirmed that Claudia's vitals were stable, then unwrapped the arm wrap and packed it away before she turned back to Patrick. 'And you must be the doctor who was in the right place today and brought this young lady's twins into the world.'

Patrick nodded. His mind was still filled with questions about Thomas and Luca's father but he needed to block them out. It wasn't his business. Claudia was alive. And now he could walk away as he should, knowing they were safe.

'Well, I'll compliment you on your skill in the baby-delivering field, which was on the six o'clock news, if you didn't already know. But you'd still do well not to criticise the rooms.' With a tilt of her head that signalled she meant business, then a wink that left them both wondering if she was serious or joking, Vanda left the room and Patrick and Claudia found themselves staring at each other, both confused by her demeanour and a little surprised at her announcement of their prime-time notoriety.

'We were on the six o'clock news?' The inflection at the end turned Claudia's statement into a question.

'Apparently—let's hope they didn't manage to find out your identity so you're not bothered by reporters.'

'I hope not,' she said, slumping back into the pillows and nervously fidgeting with her pearl earrings. Her parents had given them to her for her sixteenth birthday, while Harriet had been given a pearl necklace.

'I'll let the nurses' station and the main admissions know you don't want any interviews or fuss made of you or the boys. I'll head them off at the pass.'

Claudia looked at Patrick and thought once again he was her knight in shining armour... Or, with his modern good looks, perhaps he could be riding in on his stallion, tipping his Stetson and saving her. She hadn't even needed to ask. He just kept rescuing her. But she had to stop him doing it. She needed to save herself and her boys. Patrick wouldn't be there for them going forward. It would only be the three of them until they got back to London and Harriet returned.

'Don't worry,' Claudia replied. 'I'll let Vanda know to tell them I'm not interested in speaking to anyone. You've already done too much. Honestly, I appreciate more than anything all that you have done but you don't have to do any more. I can take it from here.'

Patrick agreed with her. He had done all that was needed and now she would be taken care of in hospital. She would leave for the UK once she and her children got clearance so there was no point in forging any sort of relationship. Romantic or otherwise.

'Here's my number,' he said, putting his business card on the tray where Claudia's water jug was placed. 'If you need anything, call me. Otherwise, I wish you and Thomas and Luca a safe trip home to London in a few weeks.' He fought the desire to kiss her forehead and stroke the soft curls away from her face. With a deep and unexpected sense of regret that he would never see Claudia again, he turned heavily on his feet and headed to the door, pausing for the briefest moment to look at the beautiful woman who had captured more than his attention that day.

Claudia wasn't sure what was suddenly stirring in the pit of her stomach and surging through her veins, making her heart beat faster, but she knew she was torn about watching him walk away. The day had been so intense but something inside of her wasn't ready to let that happen.

She knew she had to be crazy but she had to call after him.

'Please…wait,' she said then, taking a deep heartfelt breath, she continued, 'I didn't mean to seem rude or ungrateful in any way. I just mean I've put you out and I know you're a doctor and you probably have patients and…'

'Claudia—' he turned back and stopped her speech '—it's fine, really; you're right. I'm sure you can take it from here. I'm glad that you and the boys are well and through the ordeal that was today. I couldn't ask for more and I just want all the very best for the future for all of you.'

Patrick smiled at Claudia before he left but he knew in his heart her first instincts to push him away were right. There was more to the way he felt about this woman than a simple doctor-patient relationship so he had to keep his distance.

The only relationships he had were one-night stands with no strings attached and no feelings involved. And he doubted with Claudia it would be anything like that. She was already stirring feelings he didn't want to have.

It had to be just the intense experience they had shared, he reminded himself. He needed to walk away and let her *take it from here*.

CHAPTER FOUR

'SO WHAT EXACTLY are you saying is the issue with Miss Monticello's international health insurance?' Vanda demanded of the caller on the other end of the telephone. She was frowning and her cheeks were becoming flushed.

Patrick's ears tuned in to the conversation and, against his better judgement, he slowed his steps. Her serious tone caused him some concern, as did her expression as he neared the desk. The exchange of words confirmed it. He couldn't walk away and pretend he hadn't heard there was a problem. Something was driving him to want to protect the woman who he knew he should stay away from. A woman who had given him no information about herself, other than the fact she was returning to London with no explanation of why.

Questions were starting to mount in his tired mind. Was the father of her children in London, waiting for her? Or was he no longer in her life? He felt sure Claudia would have asked to call her husband or boyfriend, if she had one, even if he was away on business or fighting for his country. But she'd told him there was no one. Patrick knew he had no right to ask anything about her life that she had not willingly surrendered. Wanting to know more, let alone feeling the way he did about a woman he had known less than twelve hours, was ridiculous.

It had to stop. He knew he wanted to protect Claudia but he had to be realistic about his feelings. She was alone and he felt sorry for her. That had to be the driving force of his desire to protect her. Perhaps coupled with the desire to see her and her children safely out of hospital. He didn't want to think that there could be setbacks with any of them.

He needed to know they were safe then his job was done.

How could it be anything more than that?

'Uh-huh…okay… All right, I'll will let her know in the morning that someone from Finance will have to come and see her and make arrangements. I know she told the nurse in Recovery she was worried about the bills but we don't want her to stress. Perhaps she can extend the policy.'

Patrick looked as Vanda's expression fell further and her brow furrowed at what she was hearing. 'Oh, I see, so the twins can't be covered... Well, that's a bit of a mess but I'm sure the hospital will work something out and she'll have to pay the debt over a period of time. Yes, I appreciate it's an international policy and there are restrictions but in my ward there are no restrictions to her care.' She paused for a moment, drumming her fingers on the desk. 'No, I do hear what you're saying but please listen to my concerns.'

She continued listening with anxiety showing clearly on her face while the other staff bustled around her with the change of shift and handover. Patrick kept his focus on the conversation. She was being very polite but firm with the caller, despite her expression and the colour in her cheeks. He doubted she was the type to lose too many battles, but he couldn't help but notice she was struggling to hold her ground.

'I'd rather not. No, let it wait until the morning. Miss Monticello needs her rest and if she's stressing about hospital bills it won't help her sleep and, after what she has been through today, sleep is what she needs,' she said firmly then paused. 'I will be moving her to a ward tomorrow but tonight she's in a private room that was available. No, she doesn't have any next of kin in California or anywhere in the United States on her admission forms. She has a sister, and she appears to be her only living family, but she resides in the UK.'

With that, Patrick learnt a little more about the mystery that was Claudia's life. She had no one else in the world to call family other than her sister. Then why didn't she call her? he wondered.

'Yes, I do understand the seriousness of the situation but we will handle it in the morning. I'm back on at six,' Vanda said. She was becoming short. 'No, absolutely no. I won't budge on it. My patient comes first so please do not send anyone up now because I won't allow them in to her room.'

Patrick paused for a moment, wanting to offer assistance, but then thought better of taking over the situation. He made a mental note to have his lawyer contact the hospital administration the next day and sort through the insurance issues. After bringing the boys into the world, he wasn't about to stand by and let their mother be stressed after the fact. He tried to tell himself it was his gift to Thomas and Luca. But he knew it was not the boys alone that he was thinking about.

'I'm hanging up now,' Vanda continued sternly. 'We'll continue this conversation in the morning. There are far more practical problems to solve, like sourcing some fresh pyjamas for my patient. She'll remain in a hospital gown tonight but she has no night-dress or toiletries, not even a toothbrush, poor thing, so I can't sit around chatting to you; I'll have to go and sort out something before I finish my shift or she'll look like Orphan Annie in the morning.'

Patrick continued walking and made his way outside to the cab rank and, as he did, he sent a text to his receptionist. He needed her to run an errand for him.

Claudia woke after an uncomfortable and rest-less sleep and wanted desperately to see her babies. The uncomfortable part of her night was due to post-operative constraints but the restlessness, she suspected, was a combina-tion of anxiety for her sons and then a strange feeling of emptiness, knowing that she would never see Patrick again. She knew it was absurd to even have any sort of reaction to not seeing Patrick, let alone this feeling in the pit of her stomach. Less than twenty-four hours before, she hadn't known him and now she thought she would miss him. It was as if by meeting him she'd found a piece of the puzzle she hadn't known she had been looking for.

As she lay in bed thinking about the facts she realised how silly she was being. Fact one, she told herself, you are a single mother of twins so your life is already full. Fact two, you are a month away from being an illegal overstay in the US so you need to get back to the UK as soon as possible. Fact three, you don't trust men and never will again. Fact four, you know very little about the handsome man who delivered your babies except that he doesn't seem to want children and you have two of the most adorable children ever born. He was just checking you were all right when he visited last night, as any doctor would, she reminded herself. And he walked away. Said goodbye and good luck. That is as final and impersonal as it gets.

'Besides, it's ridiculous', she mumbled out loud. 'To even think you could miss someone you barely know.'

Her practical side forced her to push any thoughts of Patrick from her mind and blame the funny feeling in her stomach on her internal stitches or her reaction to the general anaesthetic. It had to be one or both making her stomach feel uneasy, she decided, as she pushed the nurse call button. She wanted to see Thomas and Luca as soon as possible. She wanted to hold them in her arms, if she was allowed. If not, she wanted to reach inside their humidicribs and stroke their soft warm skin and tell them that they were safe and she was there for them forever.

That they would never be apart. That she would protect them from life's harms in any way she could.

Just the way Patrick had protected them all the day before.

Her eyes were suddenly drawn across the room to the flowers. The beautiful blooms did just as Patrick wanted in brightening the borderline drab hospital room and she felt her mouth curving a little. The walls of her room were a light beige colour and the blinds a deeper shade of the same with the floor a mottled light grey. The night before she had not paid too much attention to the flowers other than thinking there was a pretty pop of colour in the room. In the morning light she could see cheerful yellow and white gerberas, a white daisy spray and blue chrysanthemums in a lovely white-blue vase, with a checked blue and white ribbon giving a pretty finishing touch. And the two small brown bears with blue bow ties. It was so thoughtful of him to have them in her room when she arrived. But then it seemed that everything he did was so considerate.

But why? she wondered. What was motivating him to be so kind to a stranger? He had already done more than could have been expected of anyone. Blinking furiously, she looked away from the floral arrangement. She had to put Patrick out of her mind. She couldn't allow herself to think of him that way. She had learnt her lesson the hard way not to trust anyone, not even herself.

The nurse, who introduced herself as Alli, arrived and unhooked the IV line. 'I'll leave the cannula in, but I'll tape it down,' Alli told her as she thoroughly flushed the tube and placed strong clear tape across Claudia's wrist where the small cannula had been placed. She was one of the youngest nurses on the ward and, Claudia would quickly come to learn, one of the cheekiest. 'Just in case you want IV pain relief during the day or tonight. Believe me, if they offer drugs, take them.'

Slowly, Alli helped her out of bed and assisted her to take small steps into the bathroom. Keeping the dressings dry, the nurse bathed Claudia while she sat on the shower chair.

'Do you have a clean nightdress?' she asked as she towel-dried her patient.

Claudia shook her head. She had no one to collect anything from her apartment and she only had oversized T-shirts, nothing really suitable for hospital. She had packed a suitcase for her trip home and only left out a pair of comfortable leggings, sweater and coat with flat boots for the flight. The other small boxes of her belongings would have been collected and already be on their way with the shipping company back to London. She had planned on shopping for pretty nightdresses for her hospital stay when she returned to London.

While she had made a few acquaintances in Los Angeles, after she'd found out the truth about her relationship with Stone and then about her pregnancy, the obvious questions that would raise had made her keep everyone at arm's length. She didn't want to make friends and then have to hide the truth from them, so she'd chosen to be alone.

'Looks like you'll be in a stylish hospital gown again today,' Alli replied as she left to retrieve another gown. Moments later, she reappeared and helped Claudia to dress. 'At least it will be clean.'

'Thank you.'

'Since they have that revealing back opening, I'm going to give you a second one to wear the other way. Like a coat to complement your stunning runway ensemble.'

Claudia smiled. Although normally she did care how she was dressed and paid particular attention to her grooming, that morning she wouldn't have cared if the nurse had dressed her in a giant brown paper bag. She just wanted to get downstairs to the neonatal nursery.

'Not before you eat, Miss Monticello,' Vanda said, walking into her room and spying Claudia in the wheelchair, ready to go downstairs. 'You'll be no good to your sons without both rest and nutrition.'

'But I want to know they're all right,' Claudia argued as she sat upright. The anticipation was building and she wanted nothing more than to be with her little boys.

Vanda picked up the breakfast tray and put it on the bed near her impatient patient, handing Claudia a small plate with some buttered wholemeal toast. Standing directly in front of Claudia and not taking her eyes from her, she said firmly, 'Thomas and Luca are doing very well. I had a call from the resident paediatrician in the neo-natal ICU about an hour ago. They're expecting you but I won't let you visit unless you've had some toast and juice. I'm quite serious, Claudia. Your body suffered a huge shock yesterday and you need to take things slowly and not forget to eat and rest, just as your little boys are doing. I'm Italian and, by the sound of your surname, so are you, so you'll know that Italians take their food very seriously. You will not get away with skipping meals with one of your countrywomen on duty. Food first, before you head anywhere.'

Just then there was a knock at the door and another young nurse brought in a delivery box with the insignia of an exclusive store on Rodeo Drive; it was about a foot long and just as wide and tall. Vanda reached out and took the box.

'Well, what's this then? It's addressed to

you. Have you been shopping online overnight, Miss Monticello?'

As Claudia took a bite of her toast, she shook her head. 'Are you sure it's for me? I couldn't afford to shop there in a mad fit.'

'Well, it definitely has your name on it, so someone's been shopping for you. I'll pop it on the bed and you can check it later.'

'P'raps it's a present from a handsome stranger because you were on TV last night,' Alli added before she left the room to continue her rounds.

'Oh, gosh, I hope not,' Claudia said as she put down the toast, as her already fragile appetite completely disappeared. 'I'm hoping no one knows my name or Thomas and Luca's.'

'With the proximity of the apartment complex and the fuss made on the evening news, viewers would probably assume you'd be here but neither your name nor your sons' were released and we've told the main admissions desk to refuse any media requests. It's our usual protocol,' Vanda replied. Then, spying the still uneaten toast on Claudia's plate, she continued, 'Would you like me to help you open the box and put you out of your misery?'

Claudia nodded as she tentatively sipped her orange juice.

'All right, here's the deal. I'll get some scissors from the nurses' station while you finish your breakfast but I won't open the box until you've had both pieces of toast and either your juice or a cup of tea.'

Claudia nodded begrudgingly.

Vanda stayed true to her word and when she returned with the oversized scissors she waited until Claudia had eaten and finished her juice before cutting through the packaging tape on the box. She opened it and handed it to Claudia.

Claudia lifted the tissue carefully. 'Oh, goodness, they're beautiful,' she exclaimed às she pulled the stunning jade-green silk pyjamas from the box.

'Very nice. Whoever arranged for those to be sent has great taste. Hold on a minute; now it makes sense…' Vanda paused for a moment, a strange look on her face.

'What is it? Do you know who sent this to me?'

'No idea, actually, but I had a conversation in handover this morning about a call one of the young nurses took from that store after I finished my shift last night. Apparently they had a phone order and wanted to check if they could deliver to a patient in our ward. They didn't say who and of course we would not have given your details even if they had asked.'

'How curious,' Claudia replied as she reached inside to find there was more. A short nightdress and a long one in varied tones of apricot and a matching floral wrap that picked up the colour palette of all of the other items and added some black trim for dramatic effect. There were also some jade satin slippers wrapped in more tissue at the bottom of the box, along with a toiletries bag. She unzipped the bag and it was filled with everything she would need.

'Was there a card?' Claudia asked, peering inside the box and then closing the lid and carefully checking the packaging. She couldn't see any sender other than the store—it had been a telephone order.

'No, it appears to be anonymous. As you said, very *curious* indeed,' Vanda replied.

Claudia put everything back into the box. 'I can't accept an anonymous gift.'

'I would—they look like silk and they're a whole lot better than your current outfit,' Alli argued as she stepped back into the room to collect the breakfast tray with a huge smile. 'I'll be back in ten minutes to take you to

Neonatal Intensive Care so it gives you time to slip into one of those stunning pieces if you like.'

Claudia looked down at the shapeless white gown and came close to agreeing for a split second but then bit her lip and shook her head. 'No. I can't.'

Vanda took the box and put it on the bed again. 'You don't have to accept it; however, you are in need of everything that's in that box, so—' she paused to put her words together '—what if you accept the gift on the condition that you will repay your generous benefactor when you've been discharged from the hospital? I'm sure you can track them down through the store.'

'I don't feel comfortable with the idea and I'm not sure I could afford to anyway.'

'Do you feel comfortable with the idea of staying in your present outfit for a few days? You'll get a fresh one each day, of course, but still the same white number with the lovely back opening! Do you have anyone who could go shopping for you?'

Claudia nodded. 'No, there's no one I can call.'

'I thought as much. You'll be in the nursery a lot over the coming days and the pyjamas and gown would be most helpful. I did manage to find you some toothpaste and a toothbrush and a few other bits and pieces but they are pretty basic and I'm sure whatever has been sent to you would be a whole lot nicer.'

Claudia once again bit her lip as she tried to put everything into perspective. 'I know I need them, particularly the toiletries, but do you really think I will be able to find out who sent the gift and repay them?'

'All I can say is that we'll do our best.'

'I *will* find them and I *will* send them a cheque for the entire amount as soon as I can. I mean it.'

Vanda left the room and Claudia slowly and carefully changed without contorting too much. The softness of the pyjama fabric felt glorious on her skin. Feather-light and cool to wear. Her body felt as if it had done battle the day before and this was a little bit of pampering.

Claudia sat down again to rest. She wanted so much to see her sons. She couldn't wait to hold them and tell them how much she loved them. Alli had not arrived so she decided to call Harriet and give her the good news about Thomas and Luca. Her sister had no idea of what had transpired over the last twenty-four hours or that she was now the aunt of two wonderful little boys. It was eight o'clock in the morning and, knowing that Argentina was five hours ahead of LA, Claudia felt confident she wouldn't wake her sister.

Harriet answered the phone after only two rings.

'Hi, sis, how are you? I miss you so much and I have *soooo* much to tell you.' Her voice then dropped to a loud whisper. 'Oh, I'm so confused. My boring, predictable as mud life has turned completely topsy-turvy. I met this man, as close to Adonis as you would find, well, the Argentinian version of the Greek God anyway...I don't know if there is an Argentinian version, to be honest, but he is so ridiculously handsome as well as intelligent and we, well, sort of had a thing, just one night, actually, back in the UK, and I never thought I'd see him again. But now I'm here in his country. He looks even better under the Buenos Aires sun than he did in London— and he was already an eleven out of ten...'

Claudia was surprised to hear Harriet sound so nervous and clearly smitten by this man but, ecstatic as she was to hear that her sister had a love interest, she was aware that Alli would return to take her to the nursery so she blurted out her news. 'I had the babies, Harriet. You're an aunty!'

'What?'

'I had my babies.'

'So early, Clau? Are you and the babies okay?' She stopped in her tracks.

'Yes, I'm fine and Thomas and Luca are so handsome.'

'Thomas and Luca! You named them after both grandfathers?'

'I hope you don't mind that I took both names in one fell swoop. I didn't leave you a grandfather for when you have children.'

Harriet laughed. 'Phuh—me? No, I don't think I'll be having children anytime soon. I'm happy you used Nonno's and Papa's names. I still can't believe you had twins! So tell me about my nephews—are they happy and healthy little boys considering they were early?'

'They're doing well, particularly since they were born in a lift.'

'In a lift?'

'Yes, a lift, or maybe I should say an elevator since I'm here in LA.'

'LA? I'm confused. I thought you were heading back to London to have the babies?'

'I was but my water broke in the elevator

and Patrick helped me to give birth. Actually, Patrick saved my life because I haemorrhaged and passed out and then paramedics rescued us all and I had an emergency hysterectomy.'

'How can you tell me you're okay with all of that going on? I need to get there now.' Harriet began pacing nervously.

'No, Harriet.' Claudia's voice was firm. As much as she wanted more than anything to have her sister with her, she refused to pull her away from the first adventure of her life. She was proud that her twin was finally jumping into something with both feet. Maybe they weren't so different after all, or maybe they were switching roles. For a while, at least. 'You can't do anything. For once you need to stick with your plans and stop trying to rescue your big sister. I'm fine, the surgery went well and I have two adorable little boys. We'll be heading home to London as soon as they're strong enough and you can meet them.'

'I need to hop on a plane and get to LA now.'

'Harriet, please listen to me. The orphanage needs you more than me. I'm well taken care of. Everything's fine here. I have a place to live until I leave for London.' Claudia had to lie or she would risk her sister doing what she always did—stepping in to save the day. Claudia had no idea where she would live. Her apartment was gone, she assumed her suitcase would have been taken down to the concierge's office, but she had barely any savings to her name and only a changeable ticket back to London. She would have to work things out quickly, but not at Harriet's expense. Her sister had finally found her dream job and perhaps even her dream man and Claudia was not taking either away from her.

'Is the ex keeping his distance? Does he know about the birth?'

'Yes, he's keeping his distance and no, he doesn't know I've had his sons. He wouldn't care. His lawyer told me he didn't want to be updated about the pregnancy. So I thought I would keep the news to myself. It would hardly have had him skipping with joy.' Claudia paused. 'His wife still has no idea that the boys or I even exist. Just as I had no idea she existed when I fell for his lines. It's amazing how he hid his marriage so well. I must be the most stupid woman in the world.'

'You're not stupid in any way,' Harriet countered softly. 'Just way too trusting for your own good. But you're better off without him, Clau.'

'I know,' she said then, thinking back to the tiny little boys waiting for her in the nursery, she smiled. 'But I have the most wonderful sons so my regrets about my relationship with that man are tempered. He gave me the greatest gifts, Thomas and Luca…and permission to *not* have him in my life. The papers arrived from his lawyer last week. He doesn't want his name on the birth certificates and waived any parental rights.'

'That's so cold!'

'He offered me a trust fund for the boys but I told him to keep his money.'

'Will you be all right without an income?'

'I'll be fine once I get back home in a few weeks. My life will be perfect…'

'I worry about you being alone.'

'I'm won't ever be alone. I have Thomas and Luca, and I'll always have you.'

'That's the truth,' Harriet agreed.

There was also someone else who had momentarily stepped into her life. Claudia was determined that in the future, when he would be just a memory, she would tell her sons as they grew up about the man who'd brought them into the world and also saved their mother's life. Even though they might never meet Patrick, they would always know about him. And how very special he was.

'I'd better say goodbye, though, as the nurse will be back to wheel me down to the nursery any minute.'

'Okay, but you call me if you need me. I can be on a plane and there with you in a few hours. I love you, sis,' Harriet told her.

'Love you too, Harriet,' Claudia replied then hung up before she had a chance to answer her sister's final question.

'Wait, who's Patrick…?'

CHAPTER FIVE

'MISS MONTICELLO, I'M Dr Wilson, the neo-natologist here at Los Angeles Mercy Hospital. I need to speak with you in private for a moment.' The doctor leant down and held out his hand and Claudia tentatively met his handshake. She had only just arrived in Neonatal ICU and had not yet seen her sons. She had no idea why he wanted to speak with her but she felt her heart pick up speed as his tone seemed quite serious. She hadn't considered there could possibly be any bad news after yesterday. The boys both seemed perfect despite what they had all been through.

What had changed?

'Please call me Claudia,' she replied as she began to nervously play with her freshly scrubbed hands and continued observing the doctor suspiciously. She tried to contain her emotions and wait for the doctor to speak but questions driven by mounting fear came rushing out. 'Are my babies going to be all right? Is there something wrong? I thought everything was fine yesterday.' She wanted to jump from her wheelchair and find them. Her eyes darted around but she could not see the boys as their humidicribs were blocked by a tall beige partition.

'Claudia, they are both doing very well, all things considered,' he returned, clearly trying to calm her down.

'What do you mean—all things *considered*?'

'I mean their delivery in an elevator and the simple fact they are six weeks early. I was going to come to your room but the charge nurse said you were on your way down here so I thought I'd wait. You can see your boys the moment we've finished speaking. I didn't want you to be anxious in the elevator.' The neonatologist, in his late fifties, had a warm smile; his hair, which was grey around the temples, and his deep brown eyes reminded Claudia of her father. Although the doctor's very contained demeanour was not like her father's passionate, gregarious Italian personality. He was controlled and that was reassuring to Claudia but she was still scared.

'Tell me, is there something wrong?' Her eyes widened as she spoke. While he had said nothing dire nor even hinted at it, Claudia had a sense of foreboding but she was trying very hard not to fall to pieces.

'There's been a small setback with Luca and I would like to talk to you about his treatment.'

Claudia's chin began to quiver with the words coming so calmly from the neonatologist's mouth. She had just been wheeled from the scrub room where Alli had helped her to put on a disposable gown over her pyjamas and suddenly she was being ushered into a small consulting room. She had been so excited to see her boys. She hadn't thought for a moment she would hear bad news. She'd had enough, she felt sure, to last a lifetime.

'I can take Claudia from here if you'd like,' he told Alli and reached for the handles of the wheelchair. 'I'll call the nurses' station when she's ready to go back to her room,'

'Certainly Dr Wilson; I'll come back whenever Claudia's ready,' Alli said gently and reassuringly patted Claudia's shoulder. 'You'll be fine, honey. Just breathe slowly and stay calm.'

Dr Wilson wheeled Claudia into the small

office and sat opposite her. His expression was stern.

'How serious is it? I need to know.' Claudia felt her stomach tie in knots and it was nothing to do with her surgery.

'Luca had a few breathing problems yesterday and that is why he was in the open bed warmer so that we could provide oxygen through an oxy-hood, or head box as we often call it. It's a small perspex box that allows babies to breathe more easily, but Luca didn't improve overnight. In fact he seemed to be struggling so I suspected a condition called PDA. It's short for a longer medical term, and I can give you more information later. I ordered an echocardiogram an hour ago to confirm my diagnosis…'

'What's an echocardiogram? Did it hurt him?' Despite her resolve to remain in control, tears began to well in her eyes but the questions kept coming. 'Where is Luca?'

'Luca is fine at the moment, Claudia,' the doctor continued in a firm but calm tone. 'The echocardiogram didn't hurt because it's much like an X-ray. Luca and Thomas are over there, where they both were yesterday.' He motioned with his hand in the direction her sons. 'The humidicrib with Thomas is beside Luca's open bed warmer and they have one nurse looking after them both. The setback at this time, Miss Monticello…I'm sorry… Claudia,' he corrected himself, 'has been confirmed by the echocardiogram and, while it's not serious and more than likely just due to his premature arrival, we need to keep an eye on Luca and you need to be aware of his condition.'

'Will Thomas develop the condition too?'

'No. There's no sign of PDA with Thomas. We're just monitoring Luca around this issue.'

'And what exactly is the problem, Dr Wilson?'

'He has an opening between two major blood vessels leading from his heart.'

'Oh, my God, no.' Claudia's hands instinctively covered her mouth. She didn't want to cry but the news brought her to the brink.

It was all too much. She'd thought bringing her babies into the world under such harsh conditions was terrifying but this was so much worse. She felt so helpless.

'Claudia, I know you must be very scared by what I'm telling you but that is why I asked you in here to talk,' the doctor continued in a very soothing tone. 'All parents have that initial reaction—it's perfectly normal—but you need to understand a little more about Luca's problem and the treatment options. The opening between the blood vessels I'm discussing is a normal part of a baby's circulatory system *before birth* but it normally closes shortly after birth. While a baby is in the mother's womb, only a small amount of his or her blood needs to go to the lungs. This is because the baby gets oxygen from the mother's bloodstream.'

'So why did Luca's not close?'

'It is probably due purely to his prematurity. You see, after birth, the baby is no longer connected to the mother's bloodstream and the baby's blood needs to go to his or her own lungs to get oxygen. When a baby is born on or around their due date the baby begins to breathe on his or her own and the pulmonary artery opens to allow blood into the lungs, and the other opening closes. But in premature infants it is not uncommon for it to remain open and a small PDA often doesn't cause problems.'

'Does Luca have a small PDA or a big one?'

'We don't know yet but if it's small then he may never need treatment.'

'But if it isn't small, what then?'

'A large PDA left untreated can allow poorly oxygenated blood to travel in the wrong direction, weakening the heart muscle and causing heart problems.'

Claudia's world just became a little darker and her own heart sank. 'Will he need surgery?' She felt increasingly powerless to do anything as she waited on tenterhooks for the answer.

'Not at this stage. His treatment for the time being will involve monitoring and medication.'

Her mind was spinning and her body reeling from the news about her baby boy. She felt so overwhelmed and unsure of where to turn. Then she realised there was nowhere to turn. She only had herself. And her little boys only had their mother. She drew a deep restorative breath and faced the doctor. She had to be strong for the three of them.

'What sort of medication?' she asked, shaking her head.

Before the doctor could respond, there was a knock at the door.

She looked over her shoulder to see Patrick standing in the doorway with the same expression she remembered from the day before. The expression that told her she would get through whatever lay ahead when she had no idea how. Her brow was lined in confusion and a single tear of relief trickled down her cheek. Quickly she wiped it away with the back of her hand.

'Claudia, I came as soon as I could,' he began as he stepped inside the room. And closer to her.

'But I didn't call.'

'No, I asked the hospital to keep me posted about the boys as I was listed as the doctor who delivered them. It was professional courtesy for them to keep me updated. I called late last night and asked to be informed if there were any problems with either Thomas or Luca. I knew, with their premature births, there may be issues and I wanted to be here for them.'

What Patrick wanted to say was he wasn't just there for Thomas and Luca. He wanted to be there for her. But he couldn't bring himself to say it. He felt certain she wouldn't want to hear it and he didn't want to say it and believe it. Having feelings for someone—wanting to be a part of Claudia and the boy's lives—was so foreign to him.

He had collapsed onto his bed after a long hot shower the previous night. After returning from the hospital, he had tried to put Claudia out of his mind. He'd hoped as the steaming water engulfed his body he would come to his senses. But he didn't. Her gorgeous face, her feisty nature and her strength in the face of pain that would have crippled the strongest of men, kept pulling his thoughts back to her. And then there was her instant love for her boys. All of it made it impossible for Patrick to push her image away. He couldn't erase her from his thoughts. He had spent hours trying but failed and gave in to what he knew he wanted to do. Against his better judgement, he wanted to be there for them all if they needed him.

Claudia felt relieved to have Patrick so close but so torn at needing him. She was confused. She said nothing as she looked at him. There was nothing in her head that would have made any sense if she'd tried to speak.

Patrick turned his attention to the doctor. 'Dr Wilson, I'm Patrick Spencer. We spoke on the phone earlier.'

The doctor stood and extended his hand to greet Patrick and, in doing so, broke the tension between Claudia and Patrick.

'Nice to meet you in person. Please call me

Geoffrey. And I must commend you in person for your medical intervention in the elevator. You wouldn't want to do all your deliveries that way, I'm sure.'

'No, an elevator delivery is not something I would've willingly opted for,' he responded with a lightness to his voice. He met the other doctor's handshake but gave away nothing more. Patrick's current medical specialty bore no relevance in the neonatal nursery. He had been honest with the obstetric surgeon when asked directly the day before, but offering up information not requested was pointless. His former medical knowledge was still very much intact, even if his career with babies was long gone.

Claudia watched the men's conversational banter with a blank expression on her face. Her emotions were a roller coaster but she still had questions about her boys that were clear-cut. Even if anything to do with her own heart and head was not close to straightforward.

'You mention drugs, Dr Wilson. What drugs are you talking about for Luca? Do they have any side effects?'

The doctor immediately returned his focus to Claudia. 'Ibuprofen will be the drug that will be given to Luca. It's an anti-inflammatory that could help to block the hormone-like chemicals in Luca's body that are keeping the PDA open. Ibuprofen could very simply allow it to close in a very short space of time.'

'Is this condition common?' Her voice was steadier and she felt as if her co-pilot had returned and was standing beside her. Still hugely confused by her own feelings, she was slowly digesting the idea that together they would navigate a problem that only moments ago she'd found overwhelming.

'It occurs in about eight in every thousand premature births but most correct themselves in a very short time frame and some in only a few hours.'

'So Luca will be all right?' she asked with her eyes still searching for reassurance, moving from Patrick to Dr Wilson and back again.

'I am fairly sure that over the next day or so the condition will correct itself,' Dr Wilson offered. 'But you still needed to be informed. I don't like to hide anything.' Claudia felt reassured to hear those words. She didn't want anything to be hidden from her ever again.

'And you agree, Patrick?'

He nodded. 'I do.'

Patrick's eyes met hers. The level of vulnerability in Claudia's eyes made him want to pull her into his arms and comfort her but he couldn't. He was providing medical advice. He had to behave as a medical practitioner and refrain from doing what he wanted to do as a man.

'I don't think we should cross a bridge that hasn't presented itself,' he volunteered from his professional viewpoint. 'Luca has a high chance of avoiding any invasive treatment so let's not overthink the situation.'

'Then I won't worry any more.'

Patrick sensed from the doctor's curious expression that he was trying to read the relationship playing out before him; he opened his mouth to speak but Patrick cut in quickly. 'Have you visited with Thomas and Luca today, Claudia?'

'No.'

'Then, Dr Wilson, now Claudia is fully versed with Luca's condition, may I wheel her over to see her babies?'

'Certainly,' the older doctor replied before he could ask anything else. Together they left the small room, with Dr Wilson showing the way and Patrick pushing Claudia's wheelchair. Patrick glanced down to see Claudia still fidgeting with her fingers and suddenly felt very protective. She lifted her face and smiled at him and a warm feeling rushed through his body.

It was as if he was where he needed to be and where he belonged and he hadn't felt that way in a very long time.

He pulled Claudia's wheelchair between the humidicrib and the open bed and then sat down beside her. The neonatologist tended to some new arrivals to the nursery and left them with the neonatal nurse.

'They both look almost red, and I can see their veins…I didn't notice it yesterday.'

'You didn't notice because you were so happy to see them alive and you were lucky to be alive yourself. I don't think you were up to focusing on the details.'

'But is it normal?'

'Yes, premature babies appear to be red as well as much smaller than you had imagined. You can see all the blood vessels through their skin because there hasn't been sufficient time to develop any fat underneath.'

'There are so many wires attached to them. Will I be able to hold them?' Claudia asked as the desire to have them both in her arms was stronger than any need she had ever felt before.

The nurse approached and shook her head. 'Not yet, but you can certainly stroke them both and that is important. They need to feel their mother's touch. While Thomas and Luca aren't the smallest babies in here, we still need to allow them to remain in temperatures stable enough to keep them both warm without needing to be wrapped up in blankets.'

'It also decreases the risk of an infection,' Patrick added as his eyes panned from one baby to the other. 'The humidity in the crib is controlled to help maintain the baby's hydration and prevent water loss. And Luca on his open bed is wearing a cap to help limit the heat loss.'

Claudia gently stroked Luca's tiny arm and prayed that Patrick was right and the problem with his heart would pass in time.

'Patrick,' she began, 'I know you said not to cross a bridge that isn't in front of me, but I can't put blinkers on and pretend there's no chance of something serious. I need to ask just one question and I want you to be completely honest with me.'

Patrick had a million questions for Claudia but he knew she might not stay in town long enough for all of them to be answered.

He accepted the simple reality that whatever time they shared in the next few days might be all they would ever have.

Their lives had collided and they had both shared the most precious and intense experience. But it was not the real world and it would all end soon enough. And one burning question in particular still resonated in the back of his mind. *Where was the man who should be by Claudia's side?*

He pushed that thought away and took a deep breath. 'Certainly—what's your question?'

Claudia looked over at Thomas inside his glass humidicrib and then back to tiny Luca. The question erred on the side of the worst-case scenario, which she didn't want to think about. But she needed to know and, if she had to, she wanted to hear the worst from Patrick. 'Can they guarantee the ibuprofen will work?'

Patrick paused, wishing he could tell her there was a written in stone guarantee but there was no such guarantee. 'No, to be honest, the medications aren't one hundred percent effective and if Luca's condition is severe or causing complications surgery might be needed, but that is not something you have to consider now. Luca's doctor seems very hopeful that the drugs will work.'

'But if they don't?'

'Claudia,' he said, taking her hands in his instinctively and, against his better judgement, he looked at the tears welling in her eyes. She wasn't looking at him any more. She was lovingly watching her tiny son but he noticed she didn't flinch or pull away and left her hands in his. He hated admitting it but there were undeniable sparks as her skin touched his. She was lighting a fire inside him where he'd thought there were only cold embers incapable of feeling any warmth ever again. 'Like I told you before, let's not worry about something over which we have no control. If surgery is needed we'll deal with it then but now is about remaining positive and optimistic about your boys and getting yourself well too.'

Claudia turned her gaze back to Patrick and then to his hands protectively holding hers. Who was this man who kept saving her? she wondered. Should she let him get close to her? He appeared to be so upfront and honest and caring but she still needed to protect her herself from further disappointment. He'd only come into her life twenty-four hours before and she really knew very little about him. There were so many unasked questions. Maybe he wasn't hiding anything but he wasn't overly forthcoming either and that worried her.

She had been promised a life by the boys' father that was just a lie. How could she be sure that Patrick was any different?

She felt herself wanting to believe in him and everything he was saying and she was feeling, but she was scared. Was it just because of what they'd shared the day before that made her feel that she could trust him? Or was it more than that? Perhaps she felt indebted to him for saving her life and her babies. She knew she had never felt about a man the way she did at that moment.

It was as if she had known him for years.

Her head was spinning. Why could she imagine herself wrapped in the comfort of Patrick's strong arms, her body pressed against the warmth of his…and his lips reaching for hers…? She shook herself back to reality. She was in no place to be having those thoughts.

It wasn't right…but it was happening. And, try as she might, she couldn't pretend it wasn't.

She had feelings she didn't understand for a man she really didn't know.

It didn't make any sense, she thought, as she slipped her hands free.

She had to channel thoughts of Harriet: what her sister would do and how she would think. She would certainly be more realistic and practical. That was how she had to behave. It had to be about her sons from now on. There was barely enough of her left emotionally to give both sons the love and undivided attention they deserved. She had to consider them in every decision she made. She needed to keep it simple, despite the way she felt herself drawn to the handsome Englishman. To her knight in shining armour.

Perhaps they could be friends.

She threw away that idea as quickly as it had arrived. The electricity she felt surge through her body when Patrick was near made *friends* untenable. She just had to manage her feelings for the short time he was around and behave as the unofficial patient of a very handsome, charismatic doctor would. However difficult that would be.

'Is there something else on your mind?'

'No, my mind's still reeling from the news

about Luca. You'll think I'm absurd if I keep asking questions…'

'Claudia, never apologise for asking questions. These are your babies and you have every right to have each and every question answered honestly and to ask it again and again if need be.'

Claudia drew breath and with a tremble in her voice continued, 'Why is only Luca affected?' As she spoke, she looked at Thomas and wondered if she had been told everything. Or if there was more she should know.

Patrick wanted so much to hold her close and comfort her. She was frightened and there was nothing as a professional he could do other than provide standard advice, albeit in an empathetic manner. For some inexplicable reason, he wanted to offer so much more but he couldn't. He had to veto the feelings that were stirring in him. And before he swept her into his arms and kissed her more passionately than he had ever kissed a woman before.

It wasn't going to be easy but he couldn't allow romantic thoughts to invade his mind and his heart. With his arms folded across his chest, he answered her. 'Dr Wilson isn't worried because Thomas doesn't have the condition now, so he can't ever have it. The opening between two major blood vessels leading from his heart closed naturally after birth. You need to understand that Thomas and Luca are fraternal twins so they are quite different developmentally in a number of ways. While they're twins, they're essentially just like any siblings so not all of their developmental conditions are going to be shared. Fortunately, this is one of them.'

Claudia was relieved to hear everything that Patrick was explaining and his calm bedside manner was alleviating her concerns. 'I have a non-identical twin sister,' she offered, as he watched her appear to relax a little. 'Harriet. She's the complete opposite of me. She's my rock. She's a nurse, quiet and sensible, always thinking about other people. We've been there for each other since our parents died nine years ago.'

'I'm sorry you lost your parents while you were still young.' Patrick had been an adult when he'd found himself alone so he could understand the overwhelming sadness that must have been Claudia's world when she lost her parents.

'It was just before our twentieth birthday, so we weren't that young, but we had been very protected, growing up in what was essentially a close-knit household. We grew up quickly. Harriet more so than me.'

'You're obviously close to her. Was there a reason that you didn't call her from the elevator yesterday?'

'She was on her way to Argentina. I wasn't sure if she was still in transit and I didn't want to worry her. I mean, there wasn't anything else she could have done except worry.'

'I suppose you're right. Have you spoken to her yet?' he asked as he sat back in his chair a little and glanced over at Thomas and Luca, both still sleeping soundly. 'Does she know she's an aunt?'

'Oh, yes, I just called before the nurse brought me down here.'

A smile crossed Claudia's face. It was the first full smile that he had witnessed. And it made her even more beautiful, if that was possible.

'Of course,' she continued, unaware of the effect she was having on Patrick. 'And, in typical Harriet style, she wanted to rush here to be with me. Drop her life to rescue her big sister. I was born first so I'm older by three minutes but she always behaves like the older, far wiser sister.'

Patrick smiled. 'So she's on her way here then?'

'Absolutely not,' she said with an expression that told him she thought he should have known better. 'I wouldn't allow her to. She's working in an orphanage and I'm not going to have her alter her plans. I'll see her at home when she finishes her work over there in a few months.'

'So you lived together back in London?' he asked and then curiosity got the better of him. 'Were you on holiday here or a work exchange of sorts?'

Claudia went a little quiet and Patrick wondered if he had asked too many questions. Perhaps he'd been too intrusive.

'You know what, forget I asked. It's none of my business. I'm here to help answer any questions you have about your boys, not interview you.'

She paused before she spoke although she hadn't intended on opening up about the details of her past. Looking at Patrick, she couldn't help but feel they had known each other for a long time. She had felt that way from the moment he'd taken off his sunglasses in the elevator and she had looked into his grey-blue eyes.

'My sister and I still share our family home. I came over here for work. I won an internship with a weekly drama series on a major network. It was a huge opportunity and I took it. Again, I jumped in with both feet like I always do,' she announced as she gently ran her finger over her tiny son's shoulder.

'I don't think jumping in is a bad idea. You experience all that life has to offer that way.'

'And some,' she muttered under her breath and felt a shiver of regret run down her body. 'Anyway, my contract is over so, as soon as the boys are strong enough, we will all head back to London. That's where I want to raise them,' she added, turning to look Patrick squarely in the eyes. 'And my leaving is something the boys' father does not object to... In fact, he is quite...' She stopped. There was no need for Patrick to know any more. 'Let's just say my leaving is not causing him any grief.'

'Well, then, we need to get them strong enough to travel.'

Patrick stayed with Claudia for another twenty minutes, then excused himself as he needed to get to his practice. He had an afternoon roster of new patients and a few post-operative.

'I'll leave you with your boys, but if you like I can call again over the next few days to check up on all of you.'

'I'd like that,' she said instinctively but the moment the words passed over her lips she knew she shouldn't have given him that answer. It was opening them both up to the inevitable.

She now had a date with a potentially sad farewell looming on the horizon.

Claudia had spent two days sitting beside Thomas and Luca, praying for them to reach the next tiny milestone and, despite the rush of hormones after the birth, she was feeling better emotionally but physically exhausted. She had stroked both boys between their gavage feeds and she chatted with the nurses and doctors. The doctor had reassured her that Luca's condition was already showing improvement and he believed that within days they might be able to stop the ibuprofen.

She had also received a call from Harriet. Her sister wanted an update on her nephews but she seemed distracted. She hadn't been disinterested at all but there seemed to be something on her mind. Claudia put it down to the tireless work she must be undertaking at the orphanage. She had nothing but admiration for her sister and could hardly wait for Thomas and Luca to meet her.

After she hung up, she suddenly felt tired and a little sore as they had ceased the IV pain relief and she was just having four hourly tablets. She decided after dinner to stay in her room and have an early night and get up early to spend the next day down in the nursery. To her surprise and relief, she had been able to stay in her private room.

She had missed seeing Patrick the previous evening and during the day and wondered if she would ever see him again. Perhaps he had done his heroic act and then disappeared into the night, she thought. Her eyes drifted to the night lights of Los Angeles that she could see from her bed and she wondered where he was. Was he thinking about her and the boys?

While he had every right to be enjoying dinner or drinks with another woman, a crazy part of her felt jealous. Was he dining at an elegant Beverley Hills restaurant or somewhere swank in downtown LA? Was his stunning date enjoying his company, laughing at his anecdotes or just mesmerised by his stunning eyes?

Was the thought of the woman who had

ruined his jacket and shirt the furthest thing from his mind?

Hesitant to overstretch, she gently moved her body to the edge of the bed so she could put her teacup back on the bedside cabinet. Then she eased back into a comfortable position and plumped up her pillow before she nestled under the covers. Thinking about Patrick and actually spending any time caring what he was doing at that time of the evening was ridiculous, she berated herself. And having flashbacks to the moment he'd removed his shirt in the elevator was borderline torturous since she knew they would never have a future together.

She looked up at the ceiling, wishing suddenly that her parents were alive to meet their grandsons. They would stroke their tiny cheeks and kiss them from morning to night and the boys would have loved their grandparents. If only they'd had the chance to meet them.

And how would her parents have reacted to Patrick? They would most certainly thank him for bringing Thomas and Luca into the world. Her father would shake his hand and then pull him into his strong embrace with a hearty laugh. Her mother would be a little more reserved but still tell him how grateful she was for what he had done in saving their precious grandchildren.

She felt a tear slip from her eye and onto the pillow.

Her heart ached for what she had lost, now more than ever.

CHAPTER SIX

PATRICK STOOD OUTSIDE the door of Claudia's hospital room, trying to resist the temptation to knock. He wondered why he had returned. He had tried to stay away and had almost succeeded. But something drove him to see the gorgeous brunette.

Was there a man who still owned Claudia's heart? Despite alarm bells ringing, he knocked on the door. Why was he going against every rule he had followed for over a decade? Never get close to someone, never form a bond or risk his heart, never look for more than one night. His decision to become an island had been born of necessity and it had served him well. But that resolve had never been so tested as it was now. The idea of Claudia, Thomas and Luca featuring in his future was a recurring thought that haunted him.

His rejection of family and his family's rejection of him were combined in fighting his thoughts about Claudia and the boys. And Claudia and the boys were winning.

'I hope it's not too late. The nurse said you were still awake.'

It was a voice that the sensible part of Claudia's brain didn't want to hear but one that made her hopeless heart do a little dance. She wiped her eyes with the back of her hand and tried to pull herself up in the bed as Patrick walked into the room. He was dressed in dark clothing and he cut a ridiculously attractive figure. His trousers were black and he had a charcoal polo top and black leather shoes. His clothing highlighted his sun-kissed brown hair and light tan and the stubble that she imagined would be soft to her touch.

His appearance was intoxicating. He wasn't fighting fair, she thought. How was she supposed to keep her thoughts to doctor-patient when he looked so damn good?

'You shouldn't have come; it's so late and you probably have far more important places to be than here.' Her voice was crisp and it belied how truly happy she was to see him. She didn't want to need him the way she did. She didn't want to repeat the mistake of thinking she knew everything about a man, only to have her heart broken by what he was hiding.

But something about Patrick made her think he wasn't hiding anything.

Was he an exception to the rule?

Patrick looked into her eyes in the dim light of the room and searched for something.

He didn't find it immediately but he persisted and moved closer to the bed.

He saw her full lips curve into a smile. And her eyes were smiling too. He found what he was looking for. Despite what she was telling him, there was a welcome on her beautiful face. Part of him didn't want to see any warmth there. He normally chose women who weren't looking for the picket fence and happily ever after because he couldn't provide it.

With one look he was reminded of just how different she was and how he didn't want to walk away without knowing more about her.

'I'm sorry I couldn't be here earlier today or last night. I had patients until late and a surgical roster today that finished about an hour ago.' There was more he wasn't saying. He had forced himself to stay away. Tried to push thoughts of her from his mind and pretend that she hadn't crept under his skin.

He had no choice but to give in to his desire to see her.

'You know there's no obligation to come. You're a busy doctor and I suppose there are lots of women having babies.' She fussed with her bedclothes and averted her gaze as she spoke. She didn't want to fall into the warmth of his eyes.

He looked at her for a moment in silence with a curious expression.

'What is it?' she asked, sensing she had said something silly but not understanding why.

'I'm a doctor, Claudia, but I don't spend my days delivering babies.'

She shot him a puzzled look. 'What do you mean—are you a children's doctor, not an obstetrician?'

While he had not articulated his specialty during labour, with the risk of raising her anxiety level, she had obviously not read his business card.

'Do you still have the card I left you in case you needed to reach me?'

'Yes, it's in the cabinet. Why?'

Patrick crossed to the cabinet with long

purposeful steps. 'May I?' he asked as he reached for the drawer.

She nodded. There was nothing personal in there.

'Here it is,' he announced, the small white card in his hand. 'You haven't read it, have you?'

Claudia shook her head. 'I had no reason to. I haven't called you.'

She put her hand out and he passed the card to her. Squinting in the soft lighting, she searched the card for his details and read the words aloud.

'Dr Patrick Spencer...cosmetic surgeon?' She collapsed back into her pillow in horror. Her arms instinctively folded across herself in an attempt to feel less vulnerable. There had to be some mistake. 'You're a plastic surgeon? You're not an obstetrician? Why didn't you tell me?'

Patrick shook his head and drew in a deep breath but, before he could begin to answer Claudia's questions, she asked more.

'Then...how did you know what to do—are you even qualified to deliver my babies?' Her voice was a little raised and equally shaky. She felt physically sick that she'd put her life and the lives of her babies in the hands of a cosmetic surgeon.

'I knew what to do because I'm a doctor.'

Claudia frowned. She felt exposed. 'Why didn't you mention that you were a cosmetic surgeon?' she asked, looking directly at him. She was angry that he hadn't told her. His announcement brought reality home. She really knew very little about Patrick and, except for the few words they'd exchanged, which had come mostly from her, he was like any man she could have passed in the street.

Only something inside had made her want to believe that he would not wilfully hurt her. *Had she done it again? Had she trusted someone at face value?*

Patrick rubbed his neck slowly and in silence. 'You need to listen to me for a minute.'

'I'm listening. Go ahead—explain why you never shared your real medical specialty with me when you were cutting free my underwear and examining me!'

Not needing to give his reply any thought because it was the truth, he answered her quickly. 'Because telling you might have sent you into a panic. The situation wasn't desirable, you were understandably anxious and the last thing you needed to hear was the man about to deliver your babies hadn't done so in over a decade. I was confident I could do it as well as anyone but you wouldn't have known that.'

'So you have delivered babies then?'

'Yes, I delivered babies many years ago and, to be honest, in the situation we were in two days ago, anyone sharing that elevator with you would have been sufficiently qualified to help. You could not have done it alone.'

With the bedclothes tucked up firmly around her like a shield, she continued. 'So these babies you delivered, were they during your training then?'

Patrick didn't want to go into too much detail but knew Claudia deserved more of an explanation. The boys were safe now but she needed to know that they had been safe the entire time. 'I was an obstetrician in the UK. I worked in the field for a number of years so that's why you and your boys were, all things considered, in safe hands.'

It made sense and it was logical but it still unsettled her. 'Why didn't you just tell me that?'

'Because it had been almost twelve years and I knew that it still would have heightened your fear. You would have worried that

I might not have been competent. I knew I could do it but I couldn't spend my energy reassuring you of the fact.'

Claudia accepted his reasoning and even agreed in part but still…

Was there anything else he hadn't told her? Was there something else she should have known?

She fixed her eyes on him intently and decided to just ask. 'So why did you change profession? Why did you stop delivering babies?'

Patrick lowered his tall frame onto the chair beside her bed. He had never wanted to tell anyone anything about his past as much as he did Claudia at that moment. He wanted to be honest about what had transpired and the future that had been so unfairly taken from him, but he couldn't. It had been locked inside for too many years to bring it up. He had moved on and so had everyone else. He would have no idea even where to start and he was worried where it might end.

So telling Claudia made no sense, he thought. He shook his head. 'I needed a change of scenery and thought I would change my specialty at the same time.'

'So you just upped and moved countries so you could surgically create perfect noses and big...' She paused and looked down towards her breasts.

'Yes, I perform breast augmentations and facial enhancements,' he admitted. He was proud of the work he performed but it had never been his dream. Bringing children into the world had always been what he had wanted to do until he'd had to walk away.

'You said it was over a decade but when exactly did you deliver the last baby before Thomas and Luca?'

Patrick felt his jaw tense. He had made his mind up not to relive that painful time in his life, so made his answer brief. 'Twelve years ago next month and it was back in the UK...'

'Why did you give up?' Claudia interrupted him as she sought to uncover a little more detail. She sensed Patrick was perhaps not telling her the entire story. His story about leaving obstetrics in England to pick up cosmetic surgery in Los Angeles seemed to be missing a piece. What was his motivation for the change? She was curious about the handsome man beside her, whose subtle woody cologne was suddenly penetrating her senses.

'Like I said, time for a sea-change and a challenge.' He felt cornered. It wasn't a lie but it wasn't the entire story either. 'You need to know that I wanted only what was best for you in that elevator. Maybe I should have told you, maybe I was right in not telling you. We'll never know now.'

'I guess we won't.'

'You're an incredibly brave woman; I hope you know that.'

'I had limited choices.' Her mood was still pensive and his compliment didn't sit well. She had been deceived by the father of her children and, while this situation was different, it felt horribly similar. She didn't like the truth being hidden from her, no matter what it was.

'You're an amazingly resilient woman. You made a conscious choice to face adversity head-on,' he replied. In a perfect world he would open up to Claudia and let her into his past. But his world wasn't perfect. In a perfect world he would still be Dr Patrick Spencer, OBGYN in the Harley Street practice he had dreamt of opening. But if compensation for his years of disappointment came in the chance meeting with Claudia, and even if it only lasted a brief time, he felt at peace with that. She had a positivity and strength that he had never witnessed before and he felt in time he would be a better man just being around her.

Not that he would have much time.

Claudia had been let down once; he didn't want to be the second man to let her down. He wouldn't make any promises other than to enjoy the weeks until she left. To be someone she could depend on during those weeks.

A rock for her.

It all sounded so logical in his head but his body had different ideas and it took every ounce of willpower not to kiss her. Not to press his lips against hers and taste the sweetness he knew her mouth would hold.

Claudia Monticello was testing Patrick in a way he had never expected.

Claudia leant back against the pillows and felt her eyes becoming heavy.

Being close to him and reacting the way she did confused her. Looking at the curves of Patrick's handsome face in the soft lighting of her hospital room, she struggled with what she knew she had to do. What she wanted to do was to find any excuse to have him nearer to her. To feel the warmth of his breath on her face, smell the sweet muskiness of his cologne and wait expectantly for his mouth to claim hers.

But what she had to do was to push him away. She had to have learned something from her last disastrous relationship. She couldn't allow herself to develop feelings for Patrick, only to find herself disappointed again. This time she had her boys to consider. Becoming involved on any level with Patrick would be risky for everyone. Not to mention pointless. She was leaving soon anyway.

Patrick watched as Claudia seemed lost in thought. 'I should go.'

'I am a little tired,' she said, agreeing.

'Would you like me to call in to see you tomorrow?' he asked as he stood.

Claudia hesitated before she replied. She was torn. 'I'm not sure that's a good idea, Patrick,' she replied in a low voice.

'I really am sorry that I didn't tell you everything outright but there was nothing self-serving about what I did, I can assure you of that.'

'It's not that.'

'Then what is it?'

'There's no point to this…to…you and me…' She stumbled over her words, unsure of how to define a relationship she didn't understand. And one that scared her.

'To me visiting you when you have no one else in the country because your only family is the other side of the world?'

'It's not that, it's just that I don't really know you and...'

'We shared a life-changing experience and, quite apart from that, I enjoy your company. It doesn't have to become complicated.' Patrick knew that wasn't entirely true. Just being near her was driving him to want more.

'I'll always be grateful for what you did, saving my boys and myself, but I'll be returning to London soon. And there's no need for you to keep me company when you have your own life.' She paused for a moment to cement the resolve in her mind. To make sure that she was doing the right thing. To remind herself that no good would come from stringing out the inevitable. Nor could she become involved on any level with a man who hid the truth, no matter how seemingly insignificant it might appear or whatever logical reason he could provide. It was a shaky point to hang her argument on, but it was all she had and she would use it.

She had to try to be more sensible like Harriet and less impetuous. And it had to start then and there. There was no time to rethink.

'You should find a nice young woman who lives in Los Angeles. Remember I have two little boys and you don't want children. You told me as much in the lift.'

'Whoa, slow down,' he said. 'You're thinking way too far ahead.'

Claudia smiled at his response. 'I have to, Patrick. I have my sons to consider.'

'And I would always consider your children. I helped bring them into the world and they are special little men. I couldn't forget about them.' It was the truth. Patrick's feelings for Claudia and her sons had grown very real. And his desire for her was equally real. 'Can you just let this play out and see what might happen?'

'No...' She drew a breath. Whilst it was lovely to know how he felt, it didn't change what she had to do. She needed to look after her boys and forget about romance. It wouldn't be in the cards for her now or anytime in the near future and he was making her feel that it could be. And *should* be.

She had to cut him free and remove any risk of her becoming attached.

'I'm sorry, Patrick, but I think it's for the best if we say goodbye tonight…for good.'

CHAPTER SEVEN

PATRICK WALKED INTO his house, feeling more alone than before he'd met Claudia. He dropped his keys by the door and decided to take a shower and try to forget her. Put everything in perspective and move on.

As he lay in his bed, looking up at the ceiling in a room lit only by the moonlight, he wondered why he cared so much.

He didn't want a future. Or a family. She was being sensible and clearly he wasn't. For the first time in more years than he could remember, he had allowed his heart to lead him.

And his desire to kiss the woman whose face would not leave his mind that night.

He had so many questions he'd wanted to ask Claudia but he hadn't. Perhaps that was where he had gone wrong, he thought as he tossed again, throwing the bedclothes free of his body, dressed only in boxer shorts. If he knew more about Claudia he might better understand her need to push him away. She had obviously been hurt by someone.

He ran his fingers through his still damp hair and looked towards the bay window of his bedroom and the full moon suspended in the clear night sky and knew it had to have been Thomas and Luca's father who had broken her heart. She had put on a brave face when she had spoken of him having no interest in his sons but there had to be more to it. Walking away from the boys' father or watching him walk away surely wouldn't have been easy for a woman like Claudia. Her family values seemed so strong.

In that case, the man who'd fathered her children must have made her fearful of getting close to anyone. But why, he wondered, would any man treat a woman that way? It didn't make sense in the way he saw the world. A man should protect a woman, and particularly the mother of his children. He should lay his life down for her and his sons.

That was what Patrick knew in his heart he would do if he had been Thomas and Luca's father.

After a restless night and the acceptance that Claudia wanted to be alone, Patrick knew he had to keep a distance between them. But there was one last thing he intended to do. He would visit Thomas and Luca one final time to say goodbye. Even though they would never remember him, he would never forget them.

And he would always remember their mother too.

Claudia showered and changed into the silk nightdress and wrap. As the cool softness of the fabric fell against her skin, Claudia wondered who had been so kind yet secretive in gifting them to her. Could it even have been Patrick? She shook the thought from her mind. He couldn't have known she needed a nightdress and he'd had no time to go shopping as he had been spending all of his spare time with her. Running a soft brush through her hair, she looked in the mirror and thought it was definitely the prettiest nightdress she had ever seen, let alone worn.

And, as soon as she could, she would be contacting the store to find a way to repay them.

Claudia was feeling physically stronger by the day but emotionally drained. Insisting a man like Patrick leave her had been a choice she hoped not to regret but one she had an uneasy feeling that she just might. But she wasn't prepared to take the risk that she might be hurt again. Not any more.

The man made her feel butterflies in her stomach whenever he was near. Dropping the brush onto the bedside cabinet, she wondered what on earth had come over her. If she didn't know better, she would think that she had developed a crush on Patrick.

'Thank goodness, he's left your life,' she muttered to herself as she put the brush into her handbag and waited on the bed for her breakfast. She could hear the clanging of the metal plate covers as the trays were being delivered in the adjacent rooms.

'Here's yours, sweetie,' the food service worker said, bringing the tray into her room. He was an older man of African-American heritage, and he'd served her dinner the evening before. He'd been quite chatty then too.

'Thank you very much.'

'You're looking happy this morning. Any reason?' he asked, a curious smile on his time-weathered but cheerful face. 'I hope it's contagious 'cos there's some biddies on this floor that don't smile near enough for me. It's like they drink vinegar not tomato juice!'

His smile wrinkled the skin around his warm brown eyes.

Claudia laughed at his words. 'I'm just looking forward to seeing my sons in the nursery as soon as I've had breakfast. The head nurse insists I eat before I'm allowed to travel downstairs so I'll eat quickly and get back down there.'

'They are very lucky little boys to have you as their mother,' he said before he left the room.

Claudia felt a lump form in her throat. That was exactly what Patrick had said when they'd met in the elevator. He had given her the same compliment and she had spat back at him something acerbic. She couldn't remember exactly but she knew it had been rude and uncalled for. She felt ashamed. Had she pushed him away unnecessarily? Had she overreacted yet again?

She also felt terribly confused. How could those few words from a friendly old man bring her emotions back to a level of chaos?

What was happening to her? Was Patrick already inside her heart and that was why the words hit home? She took the first bite of her toast and then dropped it on the plate and slumped back in her bed.

* * *

Patrick arrived at the hospital a little after eight. The heaviness in the warm morning air set the tone for the day. He had been gutted by Claudia's hasty and unexpected dismissal and had no choice but to accept he wouldn't see her again. But he would see the boys one last time.

The first patient at his private practice was scheduled for nine-thirty so he had plenty of time to visit Thomas and Luca and then head to his surgery near the corner of Rodeo Drive and Santa Monica Boulevard. He had been practicing in the ultra-modern office building for almost seven years and had no need to advertise as the post-operative faces and bodies willing to admit to having been his patients were testament to his skills. As were those people who wanted further freshening up over the years. However, he did set a limit and directed those who he suspected of addiction to cosmetic procedures to a therapist who was better placed to address their issues with body image.

The waiting list for a consultation and surgical procedures was growing but his passion for his work was not. He was dedicated and skilled but not excited. He missed that sense of excitement. The delivery in the elevator had been everything he missed about his former profession...and more.

Patrick strolled into the nursery and spoke with the attending neonatologist about the boys.

'So Luca has improved? How is the closure of PDA progressing?'

'It's looking good.' The doctor nodded as he continued to read Luca's notes on the computer screen. 'I think we'll be able to cease the medication in a day or so.'

Patrick's mouth curved to a smile as he looked at the tiny infant, dressed only in a nappy and pale blue booties that had been kindly knitted by the Mercy Hospital Women's Auxiliary.

'And Thomas? Is he still progressing?'

The doctor nodded again. 'Yes, no major problems with Thomas. There's a few milestones to reach yet, including weight gain for both of them, before they'll be discharged but they're going from strength to strength.'

'Great to hear.'

'I'll leave you to visit with them,' the doctor said and walked away to attend to another tiny patient.

Patrick stood watching over both boys. It

had been three days since their birth. Three days since he had met their wonderful mother. He wondered what their future would hold on the other side of the world and knew if things were different that he would ask if he could visit. Travel over to London and spend some time with them—and with Claudia. But that couldn't happen. He would never visit that city again.

He stayed longer than he had planned; being with them was a joy to him that was unexpected but welcome. Finally he stroked their tiny foreheads and turned to leave.

'What are you doing here?'

Patrick's gaze lifted to see Claudia staring at him. He couldn't read her expression.

'I came to say a final goodbye to the boys. You made it clear that you didn't want to see me again so I thought I'd call in and check up on them for one last time and leave. I didn't mean to stay as long as I did. I won't intrude again.'

Claudia looked closely at the man standing next to her sons. He had been watching them the way a father should look at his children. She knew their father would never do that. She had noticed the gentle way Patrick had stroked their little faces. They would never feel that love from the man who had requested she sign a confidentiality form and not mention his *involvement*.

Claudia wasn't sure if she was doing the logical thing but it suddenly felt right. At least it felt right for the next few weeks.

'Please, Patrick, you can sit a while longer if you like.'

Patrick did just that and then did it again every day for the next four days. Just after breakfast and before his day began, he travelled to the Mercy Hospital to sit with the boys and with Claudia. He still knew little about her past but whatever had happened had made her the woman she was and that was all he needed to know. Just being around her made him feel alive.

Could he possibly feel more? Could he take a chance of being a part of their little family? He wasn't convinced he would ever be ready but Claudia had made him want to believe it was possible. He tried to ignore the simple truth that his happiness would be short-lived, with her imminent return passage to London. Instead he enjoyed every moment he spent with her and refused to question the reality of what they shared and for how long it might last.

Claudia needed to stay until Thomas and Luca were discharged and that would give them even more time to get to know each other better. Perhaps if things went well she might extend her stay. He knew he was being hopeful but nothing about their meeting in the first place had been straightforward. Perhaps fate would intervene again.

Patrick smiled as he scrubbed and entered the nursery. Claudia was already with the boys and he couldn't help but let a grin spread wide across his face as he approached the three of them.

'How's my two favourite little men and their mother this morning?'

Claudia looked up at him from where she sat holding Thomas. 'We are all very well, thank you. In fact the doctor said the boys could be released before their due date. They might be ready to go home in four weeks.'

'That's great news,' Patrick said, feeling a little deflated that the three of them would potentially be leaving his life. Although he was thrilled to hear that Thomas and Luca were progressing so well, it also dashed his hopes that something might develop between

Claudia and himself. All they had now were the next four weeks. He just had to make the most of every minute.

'I have a small confession,' he said one morning as they took a walk around the hospital gardens for fresh air after visiting Thomas and Luca in the nursery. Claudia was to be released the next day and he doubted they would see much of each other after that.

'What?' she asked, feeling very relaxed in his company and equally not wanting their time together to end.

'I'm very sorry that you gave birth in the lift and all that you and the boys have been through, but I'm not sorry that you shared *my* lift that day.'

Claudia felt her heart flutter but she knew she should fight her desire to make more of it than it was. Patrick lived in LA and she was heading back to London. She had to put their relationship in context. This feeling would not lead to more. No matter what her heart was trying to tell her head.

'I'm exceptionally glad I shared *your* lift,' she said lightly, patting his arm. 'If I'd shared a lift with a pizza delivery boy none of us might have survived…or at the very least the pizza boy would have been scarred for life.'

'Pizza boys do have to deliver under pressure, so that the pizza's still hot. He might have coped.'

'Now you're being silly,' she said.

Claudia turned to see the look in his eyes. His expression was serious. Almost a little brooding.

He took her hand to draw her in. 'I mean it, Claudia. I'm glad I was there. But not just because I could help deliver your sons. I'm very glad I met you.'

Claudia couldn't agree more but she couldn't tell him that. She felt her stomach fill with butterflies at the tone in his voice, the intensity in his eyes and the feeling of his hand against her skin. It was soft and warm and it pierced through all of her defences but she didn't want to give in to how she was feeling. She didn't want to get hurt again. She had to make him believe that she saw nothing between them when in fact she thought she was close to falling hopelessly in love with him.

They arrived back at the entry door to the nursery. They both stepped back as a nurse entered and collided softly with each other. Claudia felt the warmth of Patrick's firm body against hers. A tingling sensation overtook her entire body and it took a few seconds to calm herself. She closed her eyes for a moment, not trusting herself to turn and look up into his eyes so close. As she turned tentatively to face him, his lips hovered only inches from hers and she wanted nothing more than to lean in to him a little longer.

But she couldn't. She had to put a stop to any hint of her feelings. She was leaving the hospital. She had leased an apartment the other side of town and, while it had been wonderful with Patrick visiting every day and demystifying everything medical that was happening with the boys and being there when they'd both been transferred to the nursery on day six, she had to face the rest on her own.

She would be happy if Patrick continued visiting her sons but she needed to stop fantasising about what might be between them. Nothing could become of them because she couldn't stay and explore that possibility. She belonged back in London with her only other family—her sister. She didn't want to be on the other side of the world in this city where—apart from with Patrick—she'd experienced little kindness. Her boys deserved a clean start in life and so did she. While Patrick seemed so very perfect, he was also perfectly settled in LA.

She couldn't tell all of that to Patrick. She would rather he didn't know the sordid story about Stone and hoped he would think of her fondly after she left. She had reminded herself of that every night as she lay alone in her hospital bed, wondering how it would feel with his strong arm around her. Or imagining the softness of his lips against hers when she woke in the middle of the night and all she could think of was him.

She waited until they were alone and Patrick had taken a seat beside the bed. 'There's something I need to say.'

'I'm all ears,' he told her as he stretched out his long legs and leant back in the chair.

'It's just that I'm leaving the hospital tomorrow so I guess this is the last morning we'll be spending together.'

He sat up, pulling his legs underneath the chair. 'You're leaving the hospital, not the country, Claudia. There's no need to make it sound so final.'

'It is final,' she replied. 'I've leased a place for a month…'

'You've found a place? I could have helped

you out,' he said, cutting in, a little surprised that she had found somewhere to live without mentioning it before then. He'd planned on helping her to secure somewhere or even offering a room in his own home. It was far too big for one person and he would have been happy for her to take the guest room. But it was too late.

'I think you've been too gracious in offering help so I did this alone. I found a realtor and he secured a home for me. It's a little bit further out of town but it will be fine for the next few weeks.'

Patrick could sense her need for independence so he backed off.

'I'll more than likely be visiting the boys during the day and you'll be at your practice or operating so we might not bump into each other. That's all. But I'm happy for you to call in and see the boys if you like. They smile whenever you're around.'

'I don't think they recognise me quite yet; I think it's more likely wind but I'd like to continue to keep an eye on them.'

Claudia laughed. 'That means so much to me.'

'And you mean so much to me.' As soon

as he'd said it, he knew it was too soon. But it felt natural and he didn't regret telling her.

'Please, don't. You don't know me. Not really.'

'I'd say, after what we shared, we know each other very well. We survived the most stressful situation. Surely we share a special bond.'

Claudia wished her world was different. But it wasn't.

'You're a good man, Patrick, but we can't be more than friends.'

Patrick reached for her hands and he wasn't deterred when she pulled away this time. He reached further until he had them firmly inside the warmth and protection of his own. 'We can be anything you want us to be while you are here.'

That was just it. It would only be while she was in LA. *Then what?* Claudia felt tears welling in her eyes and she couldn't blame it on hormones. Her heart was breaking just a little.

'I enjoy spending time with you,' he continued. 'There—I said it. I'm not promising anything, any more than you are. We are two expats on the other side of the world who happen to enjoy each other's company. Unless you don't enjoy my company?'

She took a deep breath. 'Of course I enjoy your company. I enjoy your company very much, but…'

'There are no buts from where I'm standing.'

'You're not making this easy.'

'No, I'm not. I think you're amazing and I think that it would be stupid to say goodbye tonight when you will be in the same city as me for the next four weeks, maybe more.'

'It seems a little pointless…'

'I disagree.' He paused over the words. 'I think we should continue to enjoy each other's company until you have to leave.'

Patrick knew that their relationship, whatever it might be, would have to end. He would never set foot back in the UK for reasons that he couldn't bring himself to share. His family were there and he couldn't see them again. Not after what had happened. In his mind it was better for everyone concerned for him to forget he'd once had a family.

'How are you getting to your new home tomorrow?'

'A cab,' she quickly replied.

'How about I take you? Absolutely no

strings attached to my offer,' he continued with even greater speed. 'I'm operating in the afternoon. So I have the morning free to pick you up and settle you in. It's your choice, a smelly cab or chauffeur driven by me?'

Claudia felt her lips curving to a smile. He wasn't giving up. 'Not all LA cabs are smelly.'

'Not all...but why take the chance?'

She shook her head a little with frustration. Why did he have to be so handsome, so charming and so persistent? 'Okay...thank you.' There were a hundred things she could have said and each one would have been closer to how she was feeling but she couldn't allow herself that luxury.

'I'll see you back here in the morning,' he told her as he walked away.

Claudia offered him a smile as she wondered what she had let herself in for. And that thought played on her mind all through the night.

CHAPTER EIGHT

PATRICK ARRIVED MID-MORNING, just as he had promised. He knocked on her door.

'Anyone here needing a smelly cab?'

'Come in,' she replied, still feeling apprehensive about spending time together away from the hospital. It became a little more frightening to be in the real world with Patrick. 'I'm nearly ready. I spent a bit more time in the nursery with Thomas and Luca as I wasn't sure if I would be back again today until late.'

'No need to rush,' he told her. 'The meter's not running.'

She came out of her tiny bathroom with a few toiletries and, as always, her breath was taken away. He looked gorgeous and she felt sure his smile could melt an iceberg. She dropped the things into her oversized handbag and went back in to brush her hair.

'The address is on the bed,' she called out. 'I wrote it down on a scrap of paper.'

Patrick crossed to the end of the bed and picked up the paper. As soon as he read the address he shook his head. It was not a good part of town. In fact, it was straight out unsafe and, despite his resolve to respect her boundaries, he couldn't let her unknowingly put herself at risk. He decided not to say anything until she had seen it first-hand. It might not be as bad as he suspected. Her independence was akin to stubbornness, and he hoped once she had seen the location she would change her mind. He typed the address into his telephone so he could get the directions. He knew the general direction but it wasn't a part of town he frequented so he would need the GPS to find the street. He waited until she emerged in a pretty sky-blue sundress. It skimmed her knees and against her porcelain skin it looked, in his opinion, stunning.

'You look beautiful, as always.'

'Thank you,' she replied with a smile.

'Shall we go?' he asked as he picked up her bag and headed for the door.

'What about the account?' Claudia asked at Administration.

The young assistant flicked through the

paperwork and then checked the computer screen. 'It's all been taken care of.'

'Are you sure?'

'Yes, your insurance company has covered you. Your sons' accounts will not be due until they leave the hospital in a few weeks' time, according to the notes.'

Claudia was relieved to hear that and Patrick was relieved she didn't ask any more questions about the insurance. His lawyer had contacted the international carrier and worked out an arrangement so that Claudia had no out of pocket expenses. But, with all the uncertainty between them, he didn't want her knowing he had stepped in to help.

They drove along with the top down on his sports car. The fresh air felt good after so long in the hospital air-conditioning. They talked about the boys and a little about Patrick's surgical roster for the afternoon and the time went quickly. As they drew closer to the street, Claudia began nervously chewing the inside of her cheek. The suburb was not what she had expected.

Finally they pulled up outside a run-down semi-detached house. It was worse than Patrick had thought it would be. He suspected a cab driver would have dropped her off without so much as a second thought so he was glad that he had insisted on taking her there. The two foot high wire fence was rusted and missing a gate and the front yard was devoid of any plants or lawn, save for the weeds that had made their way through the broken concrete. He looked over at Claudia and, while he could see her expression had dropped, she said nothing as she released her seat belt.

'You don't have to go in, you know that,' he told her.

'Don't be silly. I've given the realtor a deposit and I'm moving in today. The shell's a little worn, but I'm sure it's probably lovely inside. Besides, I'm not buying the property, I'm only renting it for a month.'

Patrick remained silent but he felt a chill run through him as they walked up the cracked pavement to the faded teal-blue house that looked as if it had not been loved in many years. Perhaps many decades. The wire screen on the security door was torn and would be useless in providing any level of security.

He watched as Claudia took the key she had been given by the realtor and, pulling back the screen door, unlocked the wooden front door and stepped inside. He followed closely, pausing for a moment to look over his shoulder at the neighbouring properties as he did. It was not a good part of town.

The house was quite dark inside for the time of day. Claudia reached for the light switch but nothing happened. They both looked up in the poor light to see the globe was missing from the hallway. An electrical cord was hanging down from the ceiling but there was no light fitting.

'I can get a new one,' she said as she made her way down to the brightest room at the end of the short corridor, which turned out to be the kitchen and was equally well worn. The floor was covered in pale green linoleum and it was almost bare, torn in more than a few places and lifting by the back door. There was a small table and two chairs but the wicker weaving was unravelling on one of the chairs, rendering it useless. The refrigerator motor was rattling and the back window looked out onto a car-wreckers' yard. There were no curtains or blinds and the hotplates on the stove were coated with years of burnt grime.

'It's only for a few weeks until the boys are ready to travel home. It's not as if I'd be bringing them here. It will just be me.'

Patrick remained silent, but he arched one eyebrow as he followed her into the bathroom. The shower was over a bath stained with rust where the water had been dripping from the tap and running down towards the drain. And the shower curtain was missing. The mirror on the cabinet above the basin was cracked and blackened in places by mildew. There was a small window of smoky glass for privacy but it too was cracked and Patrick suspected that with very little force the window would break completely.

'Let's see the bedroom,' Claudia announced, swallowing hard and trying to sound optimistic as she made her way into the larger of the two bedrooms. There was a double bed but no bedhead and a blue nylon bedspread with a faded floral pattern that couldn't mask the dip in the mattress. A free-standing oak stained wardrobe that had one door slightly ajar stood by the window. The dirty cream-coloured net curtains covering a stained blind sagged where they were missing hooks. Claudia crossed the dark brown shaggy-carpeted floor to close the wardrobe door and discovered that the handle was broken. 'I'll be living out of my suitcase anyway so the door doesn't matter. I'm not about to be picky,' she said.

'Claudia,' Patrick began in a serious tone, 'you can't be considering living here.'

'Of course I am. I backpacked around Europe in my late teens. It'll be an adventure just like that,' she replied as she walked towards the front door, noticing there were holes in the plasterboard that looked as if someone had put their foot through the wall. 'Shall we get my suitcase so I can settle in and you can get back to the hospital? I know you have surgery this afternoon.'

'So you're moving in?'

'Yes.'

'Then I'm moving in too; we'll be house mates. I backpacked around Europe in my late teens too, so I'll share the adventure with you,' he announced. 'Let's go take a peek at my room. I hope it's as nice as yours.'

'You're not living here; that's ridiculous.'

'And you don't think you living here is ridiculous?'

'No, that's different.'

'Not in my opinion. If you move in, then we'll do it together and both risk our lives and general wellbeing!'

Claudia shook her head and narrowed her eyes at him before she walked across the narrow passageway behind Patrick to the darkened room. Reaching for the light switch, Patrick discovered it didn't work so he used the light of his phone to see the room. It was smaller and there was a single bed and what looked like a grey chest of drawers. He walked across to the window and lifted the blind to allow them to see the room properly. It took him three attempts to lift the damaged blind but when he did he could see another short electrical cable hanging down from the ceiling. There was no light fitting and again the globe was missing.

'Looks like we both need light bulbs when we head to the store.' He patted the bed, not daring to think about how many years the faded orange bedspread had gone without washing. It was stained and frayed in places along the hemline. Then he noticed the chest of drawers was actually a filing cabinet and he walked over and pulled open the top drawer. 'Great, I can keep some of my patient files in here to work on in the evenings.'

'Don't be awful. You're teasing me now.'

'Not at all. If it's good enough for you, then it's good enough for me.'

'You're being stupid. You don't need to babysit me.'

'I'm not thinking of babysitting. In this part of town my role would be more bodyguard.'

Claudia put her hands on her hips and shook her head. 'It's not that bad. I used to drive through here on the way to the studio every day. I never saw anything untoward happen.'

'And what time was this exactly?'

'What do you mean?'

'I mean did you drive through this street after dark?'

Claudia thought back. 'Not dark but early evening and early morning.'

'Then you and I will spend one night here together and if everything is fine then we'll discuss it again but I think you'll find that after the sun goes down this isn't a nice place to live. There are gangs in adjacent areas.'

'I have an idea. Why don't I ask a neighbour, or the business out the back? They'll tell me what it's really like.'

Patrick ran his long fingers through his hair in exasperation. Claudia was as stubborn as she was beautiful and intelligent. 'Let's ask, but if you get the answer I expect then I hope you agree we should just leave.'

Claudia didn't agree to anything. She showed no emotion as they walked out of the house and along the sidewalk beside the fence to where they found the owner of the wrecking yard locking up for the day. He was pulling the tall wire fence closed and securing it with a heavy padlock. Claudia picked up speed so he didn't leave before she had a chance to speak with him.

'Excuse me,' she called out. 'I'm wondering if you could tell me a little about the area. I'm thinking about renting the house that backs onto your property.'

Patrick watched as the man's face fell.

'Listen, lady, do you see the two dogs over there?'

'Yes,' Claudia answered, looking at the two heavy-set black guard dogs that were chafing at the bit, waiting for their owner's signal to begin patrolling the yard.

'They're not here for their good looks. There's not enough money in the world to make me live in this neighbourhood.' He tapped his watch with his grubby fingernail. 'Three o'clock every day I'm outta here. I've got some clients that look after the yard, if you know what I mean. I work on their cars and they make sure that my yard and my dogs are still here in the morning.'

'Perhaps the dogs will look after me too.

They'll scare away anyone who thought to break into my place.'

'Not a chance unless you want to live in my office. Sorry, miss, but you're on your own if you move into that house. You'd be dead crazy if you did.' He signalled to the dogs before he climbed into his utility and drove away. Immediately the dogs rushed towards the wire fence, gnashing their teeth and making Claudia jump back nervously.

'So do you think you need a second opinion or can we leave now and find you other accommodation? Unless you want to wait and ask a not so friendly gang member his opinion.'

'Okay, I get it. I suppose you may have a point,' she said with a decidedly sheepish look upon her face.

'May have?'

'Fine, the man confirmed your suspicions about the suburb. And I concede the house is not as nice as the realtor described on the phone. I can't believe he lied to me.'

Patrick didn't comment. There was nothing he needed to add except to ask her to get into his car while he locked up the house.

A few minutes later they were on the freeway and heading towards Beverly Hills. 'I'll only stop at your home long enough to make some calls and secure another short-term rental,' she told him. 'I can make a reservation in a hotel tonight if necessary.'

'Whatever you think is best, but my home is big enough for both of us.'

'Thank you, Patrick, but I won't get too comfortable. I'll be leaving in a few hours.'

It was only ten minutes on Freeway 405 and then three miles on Wilshire Boulevard before Patrick turned into a street lined with towering palms. The sweeping grounds of each of the palatial homes was perfectly manicured, and small gardeners' vans were dotted along the street with men in wide-brimmed hats busily planting and trimming the gardens. They drove a little way to a slight bend in the road and then slowed. Heavy black electric gates slowly opened and Patrick drove the car inside and the gates closed behind them.

He drove the car up the driveway to the front door of the double-storey white stucco mansion he had called home for two years. The property also boasted a tennis court, a heated swimming pool, spa and a four-car garage but Patrick didn't mention any of it. Cosmetic surgery had been kind to him, he admitted, but equally he had worked hard in his new field and had been recognised as one of the best by Hollywood's very particular clientele.

He helped Claudia out of the car and then opened the front door. 'Please go in; I'll get your bag.'

'I won't be staying,' she reminded him. 'Perhaps you should leave my things in the trunk.'

He smiled to himself. He wondered again if she had always been that fiercely independent or had circumstance made her that way? But, whatever the case, he understood she had every right to want to make her own decisions. He just hoped they didn't include another dubious choice of realtor.

'I'll get your belongings in case there's anything you need.'

Claudia spun on her heel to take in the magnificent surroundings. The foyer had a large atrium with a stone water feature. The sound of running water echoed in the large open space. Looking past that to outside, she could see more gently moving water. It was, she assumed, an endless pool and a panorama of the Hollywood Hills formed a backdrop.

'I will let you find your way around. The

guest bedroom is on the ground floor, third door on the left, if you'd like to have a shower or a lie down. It might do you good to rest for a while. I can take you back to the hospital to visit the boys this evening.'

'You're being too kind. And too generous. It's unnecessary, honestly.'

'Claudia, it's a big house. I live here all alone and you're most welcome to stay here until you leave. I'd rather you were here than making *friends* in that neighbourhood! And, by the way, never recommend that realtor unless you really dislike someone,' he said with a wink before he closed the door and left her alone.

Claudia was more confused than she had ever been in her life.

The most handsome, kind, considerate man wanted her to live with him. She owed her life to him. And she wanted to be with him more than anything, but she couldn't. He had made it obvious he had feelings, not only by opening his home but also the way he kept reaching for her. But she wasn't ready to take that leap of faith and trust again. He was a kind man and as much as she wished he was the father of her sons, he wasn't. And she couldn't risk them all falling in love with

Patrick. What if he walked out one day—the way that the boys' father had done? And turned her life upside down.

She had to be sensible and see the world the way Harriet would. Put a practical filter across her decisions and stop being led by her heart.

Certain and confused in equal amounts, she found her way to the guest bedroom and, kicking off her shoes, she sat on the bed. She suddenly felt a little tired and the bed felt very soft and comfortable so she thought she might just lie down for a moment. She told herself that she wouldn't fall asleep but just close her eyes for a moment, then she would call another realtor and find another short-term lease. And that night she would stay in a hotel.

Patrick came home to a darkened house but in the light from the porch he could see Claudia's suitcase still lying against the wall in the hallway. He turned on the lamp in the living room, unsure if she was at home or had caught a cab to the hospital. Quietly, he walked through his home and found her asleep on the bed. While it was still warm outside, the air-conditioning had kept the house cool and she was wearing a thin sundress so he pulled the throw rug up over her and closed the door. She was exhausted and he had no intention of waking her so he put a call through to the hospital to check on the boys. His call was connected to the neonatal resident.

'Dr Spencer, I've just finished reading the boys' notes for today. I did try to call Miss Monticello but had no luck getting through.'

'It was a big day for Claudia and she's taking a nap now so that's why I've called. I will pass any updates on to her.'

'Thomas is still progressing well, as he did from day one, and Luca's PDA appears to be self-correcting. He'll be having another echocardiogram tomorrow but Dr Wilson is confident no further treatment will be required. So please let Miss Monticello continue to rest. She can come in the morning to see them. Both boys are asleep and will have their gavage feed in another two hours. There's no need for Miss Monticello to be here when the rest would do her more good.'

Patrick thanked the young doctor and hung up the telephone before he ran upstairs to change into shorts and a T-shirt. He would take a dip in the pool later but first he would cook some dinner for the two of them. He knew it was stupid to think there would be anything between them after the next few weeks but she was getting under his skin and he couldn't deny it.

For some inexplicable reason, he didn't want to let the dim future get in the way of a happy few weeks.

Life was short and so he intended to enjoy whatever time he could with her. She challenged him and just being around her made him feel alive. Her accent and her very British mannerisms surprisingly made him think almost fondly of London and even fleetingly of his family. And, in a deep dark corner of his mind, he thought perhaps there was a chance, however slight, that she could change her mind and stay in the US.

Claudia woke to the smell of cooking. Her eyes struggled to focus and for a moment she forgot where she was until suddenly it came back to her. She had lain down for a moment in Patrick's guest room. It was dark but she could feel the light weight of a throw rug over her. She didn't remember pulling it up so assumed Patrick must have returned home and covered her. The curtains were billowing with the cool evening breeze and there was light creeping under the now closed bedroom door.

Suddenly she sat bolt upright. She hadn't called a realtor. She reached for her phone and discovered it was after six, in fact closer to seven.

'Darn, bother, you silly cow,' she said as she rubbed her forehead and silently continued berating herself for falling asleep. Now she would have to find a hotel as soon as she had visited Thomas and Luca. She swung her legs down and felt around for her shoes before she headed in the direction of the light. She would thank Patrick for his hospitality and get a cab to a hotel, check in with her bags and then head straight to the Mercy.

There was no way she could accept his hospitality. Their relationship had already overstepped the boundaries of common sense.

Moments later, Claudia stood in the doorway to the kitchen, watching Patrick stirring something that smelt delicious on the stovetop. Suddenly her heart felt lighter. But her head felt terribly confused. He turned to see her watching him and she felt very self-conscious. A tingling sensation crept up her neck and onto her face and she felt certain the blush had spread across her cheeks.

'Well, hello sleepy-head. Did you have a nice nap?'

His eyes twinkled as he spoke and she tried to ignore her increased heartbeat.

'I did, thank you, but you should've woken me. I slept for far too long. I need to get to a hotel and then see the boys.'

He lowered the heat underneath the pan and turned around to face her. He was wearing a tight white T-shirt and cargo shorts. His toned physique was cutting through both. His feet were tanned and bare on the large terracotta tiles.

'I've checked on Thomas and Luca and they are both doing very well. They were sleeping when I called but,' he said, glancing at the roman numerals of the large wall clock and then back to Claudia, 'they will have been fed again and should be tucked in again for another four hours or so.'

'I should have been there for that feed.' She was angry and disappointed in herself. She was convinced her boys needed her more than she needed sleep.

As if he sensed her self-reproach, he added firmly, 'You can't do everything, Claudia. The rest you had this afternoon was important. In fact, I told the neonatal unit that you wouldn't be back to visit the boys until to-morrow.'

Claudia was taken aback by his announcement and she felt her body tense. 'Why would you say that to them without asking me? Whether I see my sons or not is not your decision to make.'

'Well, in my capacity as a doctor it is. You need to get your own strength back, as I have said to you more than a few times. You'll be no good to your sons if you run yourself into the ground the first day out of hospital.'

'But I want to be with them.'

He shook his head and turned back to the stove. While he admired her strength, he found her stubbornness in ignoring her own wellbeing frustrating.

'I'm all they have in the world.'

There it was again. Her reference to Thomas and Luca having no one but her.

Patrick nodded his understanding of her need to be with them but he wanted to at least get some food into her so she could keep up her strength. 'Then I'll take you there after dinner.'

'There's no need for you to take me. I can do it after I book into a hotel.' Her arms were crossed across her chest and her eyes were narrowed.

'Claudia, I know you have a need for independence above all else, but you have to look after yourself. And since you don't seem to understand the importance of taking care of yourself I'm more than happy to step up to do the job.'

'I'm perfectly capable of looking after myself and my boys on my own. I'll be doing that when I return to London in a few weeks.' She felt her neck tense with the thought of depending on any man again.

Her words cut through him like a knife. He wasn't sure if that was her intention but, if it was, she had succeeded.

'Point made,' he replied as he returned to the task at hand. Listening to his heart had been something he'd successfully avoided for many years and it appeared, from Claudia's reaction, it was something he needed to continue avoiding.

Disappointment suddenly coloured his mood. The heat was still under the large pan of boiling water so he dropped in the fresh pasta. 'If you want to share dinner before you grab a cab then you're welcome. If not, then

I can help you out with your bag when the cab arrives.'

Claudia looked at him as he turned his attention back to preparing dinner and wished they had met under different circumstances. Before she had been so badly hurt and disillusioned. He appeared to be everything she'd once dreamed of finding in a man...but she was no longer looking and she doubted she ever would again.

He turned back to her for a moment. 'I don't want you to feel pressured, Claudia. That was never my intention.' His reply was truthful, his voice gentle and low—almost a whisper. 'I just wanted to help you...but I would never force you to do anything or stay anywhere you didn't want to be.' His voice trailed off.

Claudia wasn't sure how to respond. He had been a gentleman up to then and she doubted that would change...unless she invited him to alter his behaviour towards her. She started to wonder if perhaps she had overreacted. Once again since meeting him, she had been rude.

The first time had been due to her aversion to men and now, looking back, she knew he didn't deserve to be punished for another man's mistake. At the time she couldn't seem to help herself. But this time it was something else driving her to push him away. It wasn't his fault she was starting to have feelings for him. She wished she had Harriet on speed dial to give her logical, solid advice but it would be selfish to pull her sister away from something far more important in Argentina to ask her whether she should stay for dinner, stay the night or stay for a month.

No, she had to do this alone. She had to make a decision not based on another man's behaviour or her own doubts and insecurities. She had to make a decision based on Patrick's behaviour. And that had been nothing other than exceptional.

Just as exceptional as his broad-shouldered silhouette looked while stirring the delicious-smelling pasta sauce.

'If the invitation is still open, then perhaps I'll stay for dinner. But only for dinner.'

CHAPTER NINE

As CLAUDIA HUNG up her clothes in the walk-in wardrobe she prayed she had made the right decision. This was the second time she had rushed into moving in with a man she barely knew. Her life had changed so completely in the time since she'd arrived in Los Angeles and not much of it had been for the better, except for the arrival of her sons. She longed to return home. To where she felt life was a better fit and to where she felt a sense of family. Her internal compass was directing her back to London.

But she had unexpected mixed emotions about Patrick.

Where did he fit into her life? Would he be a part of it once she left Los Angeles or would he become a memory? A sweet memory, but nothing more.

Claudia had tried to think logically about

moving in. They had only known each other a short time, but she and Patrick had a bond that she knew she would never share with another man. He had brought her sons into the world, saved their lives and saved hers as well. He was a brilliant obstetrician and while she wondered why he had not continued in that line of work, it was not her place to question him.

Was the fact he too was of English heritage a deciding factor in her feeling comfortable enough to move in? she wondered. Did he remind her of home? Did that make her feel safe? She prayed it wasn't a false sense of security.

There had been absolutely no pressure from Patrick over dinner; in fact he had even suggested a couple of hotels near the Mercy Hospital for her to stay in that night. His lack of insistence that she stay in his home but his genuine offer made her feel more comfortable to accept his invitation. And to apologise for being rude.

Everything happening in her head, and her fear of accepting Patrick's help, was her problem to deal with and in no way related to him.

'I will pay you exactly what I would be paying at a hotel,' she'd told him as they'd put the dishes into the dishwasher and sat down in the living room.

'The going rate for a hotel around here is just over a dollar a night.'

'Beverly Hills certainly isn't as expensive as it's alluded to be,' she joked. 'In all seriousness, I must insist…'

'Here's my business proposition,' he interrupted as he looked into her eyes, melting her heart a little further. 'Since I arrived in the US I haven't been able to find my favourite English toffee with almonds. It's amazing and nothing comes close. The almonds are toasted and the toffee's covered in dark chocolate. If you manage to find some, we'll call it even. Perhaps even arrange some to be shipped over after you return home. It used to be available at Harrods. There's no deadline, just a promise that one day I'll get my toffee.'

'English toffee in exchange for living in a home this beautiful?' She turned her head and, from her seat on the sofa, she surveyed the beautifully decorated room. It was elegant but simple. It wasn't stark but nor was it cluttered and the colours were warm earthy tones and the lighting softly added a glow to the room.

'You don't like the terms? Too steep?' he

asked, staring into her eyes when they came back to meet his gaze. His lips curved to a smile and softly lined the stubble-covered skin on his jaw.

His voice sounded like the warm dark chocolate he was describing as the words flowed from his lips and Claudia involuntarily bit her own. Her heartbeat picked up unexpectedly and she closed her eyes and tried to blink away thoughts she was having about her landlord. He was far too gallant and handsome for his own good and most definitely for her own.

The French windows onto the balcony were open and the warm July breeze felt wonderful after the hospital air-conditioning so she carefully stood up and made her way to the door. Each day the physical scars were healing, but she just wished the emotional scars inflicted by the city would fade as quickly.

At that moment she needed to move away from Patrick, and the feelings she was having, being so close to him. She needed to step outside and clear her head in the balmy night air. She looked over the balustrade to the moonlight on the gently moving water of the pool. It was a perfect evening. The perfect house. The perfect man.

But, in Claudia's mind, she was so far from perfect.

And life for her had never been perfect.

Patrick watched Claudia from his vantage point on the sofa. Her feet were bare and her short hair was gleaming in the moonlight. She seemed so at peace with the world at times, but at other times almost tortured. And so vulnerable. He had to control the urge to step behind her, pull her into his arms and tell her that everything would be all right. Protect her from whatever had hurt her or could in the future.

But he had no clue what the future held for her or for him. He barely knew anything about Claudia's past, apart from her losing her father and mother. Where had she gone to school? What had made her take the position in Los Angeles? And why didn't the father of her children want anything to do with them…? But, strangely, nothing about where she came from mattered to him any more. It wasn't her past, her family or her career that made him want to be with her. It was her attitude to life. Her strength. Her independence. Her beauty.

And her love of her children.

* * *

The next morning Claudia woke early and dressed in the shorter of the two nightdresses before making her way to the kitchen for breakfast. She thought she would make something to eat for them both and then head in to change before Patrick rose. Cooking breakfast would be her way of repaying his kindness.

But he was already up. And he took her breath away. Standing at the bench with a knife in his hand, he was cutting vegetables and fruit and placing them into a large glass bowl. Nearby was a small high-tech food processor. But her eyes were drawn to his bare chest and his low-slung shorts. Swallowing and trying not to stare at the perfection of his body, she looked out onto the patio, where she could see a gym bench and weights.

'Good morning, Claudia. I hope you slept well. If you need more covers or anything just let me know.'

She coughed to clear her throat. She needed to be polite and meet his gaze but that meant looking at his half-naked body again and worrying about her clothing being a little skimpier than she would normally choose.

Ordinarily, that would not be a problem, but Patrick had to remain in the generous landlord category and she had to stay inside those parameters. She couldn't afford to entertain fantasies. She vigorously rubbed her arms as if she was cold. She wasn't. His presence was making her hot and self-conscious.

'Good morning,' she managed, trying to look around the room and avoid the obvious. Gorgeous, jaw-dropping Patrick, with both a body and smile to die for. And, first thing in the morning when most were struggling to open their eyes and look human, he was poster perfect. 'So you've been working out.'

He smiled back. 'Yes, I like to get up early and start the day using the outside gym. There are deck lounges out there so be my guest today and enjoy the stunning weather.'

'Stunning…weather.' She found it difficult to look at him and not have her eyes wander over his body in appreciation.

'I'm making a health blend with kale, carrots and a bunch of fruit. I didn't want to turn it on until you woke up since it sounds like a small lawnmower,' he said with a smile. 'Would you like one—I've prepared enough for both of us.'

'I'd planned on getting up early and cooking for you. You're already done so much for me.'

He shook his head as he crossed to the sink and washed the stickiness of the fruit from his hands then he slipped on a T-shirt that was hanging over the back of the high-backed kitchen chair. 'I'm always up at the crack of dawn in summer and I like a liquid breakfast after a workout. It gives me energy to face the day and I've got a full day of surgery scheduled so this will keep me going. Will you join me?'

Claudia was relieved that he was partly covered and her breathing had slowed accordingly. 'I'd love to, thank you.' She sat on a chair near to the bench where he was working and thought she would steer the conversation towards his work. 'So what surgical procedures are on today? Which starlet is going double D?'

He was dropping the chopped fruit in to be blended but paused to answer her question. Both of his lean hands rested over the top of the machine as he looked at her. 'I have two post-mastectomy reconstructions. A young mother in her early thirties and a slightly older patient who just celebrated her sixtieth birthday.'

Claudia felt so stupid. 'I'm sorry.'

'Don't worry; everyone does it…'

Shaking her head in frustration at herself, she continued. 'Just because everyone thinks the same way doesn't make it right. I was condescending and I made a sweeping generalisation. I'm so stupid for saying that. I should have known there would be more to your practice.'

'Thank you. Most people just shrug and don't apologise so please don't feel bad.' He paused for a moment. 'And, to be honest, I do my fair share of purely cosmetic augmentations. The holy grail of boob jobs, the double Ds and a few Es. Those surgeries allow me to perform the worthwhile ones at a much lower cost.'

'That's wonderful.'

'Well, I have a lovely home. Don't go putting me up on a pedestal.'

Despite what he said, in Claudia's mind he was a true gentleman and already up on a pedestal and she doubted he would fall off anytime soon.

One morning after Patrick had left for work, Claudia thought she would sort out the matter of the generous benefactor before she left for the hospital. She found the delivery docket in her purse and called the Rodeo Drive store. She was determined to repay the stranger's kindness and at the same time ensure she was not in their debt.

'I'm sorry, madam, but I can't divulge the sender's details. As with all of our account holders, they're a highly valued customer. This is an awkward situation and I would truly like to help but store policy won't allow me to do so. However, you are very welcome to exchange anything that you don't like or need in another size.'

'No, I don't need to change anything. It's all perfect.'

'We do pride ourselves on the styling and quality of all of our garments.'

The young woman's delivery was very eloquent and her tone leaning towards pretentious but Claudia knew that came with the location of the store. She bit the inside of her cheek. She wasn't going to accept the gift. She had to repay the sender but she needed to think of a way quickly before the young woman ended the conversation, no doubt politely, but, however it ended, her chance to repay her benefactor would be over.

'I have an idea,' she began in an equally

polite tone, hoping to sway the sales assistant to agree to the thought that had popped into her head. 'Could I buy a gift certificate to the same value as the gift sent to me and you could mail that to them? If they have an account then you would have their mailing address. You are not breaking confidentiality because their details have not been given to me and you have just doubled your sales because they will have to visit your store to spend the certificate.'

There was no answer for a moment and Claudia assumed the sales assistant was considering her proposal. 'But they may want to know who sent it.'

Claudia wondered at the slight double standard when it came to account holders and mere mortals.

'That's fine. I don't have any problem if you let the sender know it was from me. In fact, I would be happy for them to know I had repaid the gift.'

The deal was done. Claudia gave her credit card details over the phone but the amount was even more than she had imagined. But, since she wasn't paying rent, she could afford it. There was nothing more she needed to buy for herself. She drew a deep breath at how extravagant the anonymous benefactor had been and would be hand-washing everything, hoping that it lasted for a few years, knowing what it had cost.

Claudia watched her little boys grow day by day, week by week. She was able to hold them and bottle-feed them and on the twentieth day they moved from the neonatal nursery into the general nursery. The warmth and serenity that she experienced every time Claudia held them made her happier than she thought possible and she didn't want them to be out of her arms. As she touched their soft warm skin and looked into their big trusting eyes she knew her life was complete. There was nothing she wouldn't do or give to Thomas and Luca for as long as she lived. Each milestone they reached in weight or developmental markers made her heart sing. She could imagine decorating Christmas trees with them and watching the joy on their faces as they unwrapped their birthday presents.

The boys' little faces filled out a little more every day and she could see subtle differences. Thomas was a little bigger and his mouth a little fuller and his mop of hair was thick and straight, while Luca's hair was curly and he was a leaner baby. Whether that had anything to do with his initial heart problem, she was unsure.

Claudia would arrive first thing in the morning at the Mercy Hospital and leave just after the sun set as the boys had settled into a routine and were ready for sleep. They had two feeds during the night, one at eleven and another at three in the morning, but the nursing staff insisted she get rest and come in the morning. The first time she was allowed to bathe them one at a time she had tears of joy in her eyes that fell from her cheeks into the tepid water. She was so nervous as she supported their tiny bodies in the water and then gently let the water splash over them before she wrapped them in a soft white towel and held them for the longest time.

When the weather cooled just a little so it wasn't too extreme, Patrick suggested a picnic outside for the four of them. At first Claudia was uncertain but when he walked her downstairs she caught sight of the checked blanket on the ground, complete with picnic basket, she nodded her approval. Together they collected the boys after their feed and took them down to the shady place beside the small pond. The sound of the water trickling over the rocks and running into the pond filled with oversized goldfish was relaxing.

'I think they'll enjoy fishing.'

'And what makes you think that?'

'It's just a feeling I have.'

Patrick didn't want to say that if they were his sons he would teach them about fishing, the way his father had, and they would learn to love it as he did.

Claudia watched him fussing over her sons and she had the feeling that, despite what he said, he would be a wonderful father.

The basket was brimming with wonderful picnic food; there were assorted sandwiches. It truly was a family outing. Whatever family meant, moving forward.

Claudia took photos of the boys with her phone camera every day as they grew. It would be a reminder of how far they had come and a keepsake for them when they were older. She decided to have a photo of each of them framed for Patrick. He had been so wonderful and she wanted him to have a memory of the little boys he had brought into the world. It saddened her that soon they would be worlds apart but it was a fact she had to accept.

She stopped at the drugstore on the way

home one day and had two of the cutest photos printed and bought two silver-plated frames. And as she walked into his bedroom that afternoon to place them on the dresser as a surprise, she felt strangely at home. The room had a masculine feel to it but it was also warm…and inviting. It was decorated in muted warm tones of grey. Heavy deep grey drapes framed the window and the softest pale grey carpet covered the floor. The bed and bedside cabinets and the dresser were black and there were three large charcoal drawings on the wall behind the bed, also framed in black. The bed cover was the same tone as the drapes. It was a simply decorated room but stunning. The longer she stayed, the more she felt at home. She would have preferred that she felt like an intruder but she didn't.

Placing the frames on his bedside table, she left the room, her eyes surveying one final time where he slept every night. She wondered if his bed was as soft as hers and if he slept on his back or on his side. Did he toss the covers off or did he sleep peacefully…?

Every few days Patrick would stop at the hospital to check up on the three of them. And each time he did, Claudia felt her heart flutter as she watched him tenderly hold one of her sons. She couldn't help but notice that he was completely and utterly consumed by whichever baby he was given. He didn't take his eyes away for even a minute and he spoke to them in great detail as if they understood every word. Claudia had to remind herself that he was not their father. He gave such attention and love to them, it was often difficult for her to remember that simple fact.

Patrick gave her the use of his silver imported SUV to travel to Mercy Hospital. He knew it would help her to feel independent by not asking to be dropped off or catching cabs at all hours. He wanted her to feel the freedom she needed but still feel a sense of belonging. And it worked. She was extremely grateful to him but he did not exploit that gratitude in any way. She initially refused, as he expected she would, but when he pointed out the safety of late night trips back from the hospital she reluctantly agreed. But she insisted on putting in the gas and having it washed each week.

She cooked dinner for him two or three nights a week. And he continued to rise early and make smoothies in the morning. Occasionally Claudia would eat at the hospital so she could stay a little later with Thomas and Luca. And Patrick made Friday night their night together at the hospital. He brought fish and chips from a store owned by an expat from North Yorkshire who had relocated to LA and opened a café on Melrose. The shop was always busy and he would line up for thirty minutes just to place his order. Then Claudia would meet Patrick downstairs in the visitor gardens to eat their fish and chips together. It felt so good for both of them to step outside. They had enjoyed four Friday date nights and they were planning the fifth, the date they both knew would be the last. Claudia would be heading back to London in less than a week and, while she was looking forward to returning home, she realised leaving Patrick would be one of the hardest goodbyes she would ever have to say.

But she had no choice.

As they sat together on the patio at home one evening, Claudia sipped on her iced tea and looked up towards the stars, wondering if her parents approved of the man sitting beside her. She felt certain they would and it made her want to be honest with him about something they had never discussed.

She curled her bare feet up under herself and turned to him.

'Is there anything you want to know about me? I mean, I've been living here and you've never pressed me about anything.'

'You have a sister, whom you adore. And she's over working in South America. And you worked in television.'

'What about the big elephant in the room? The one we've walked around since we met.'

'And that would be?'

'The fact you've never asked me anything about Thomas and Luca's father.'

He studied her for a moment. 'It's not my place, Claudia. I've just thought all along, if you want to tell me you will but if you don't then I respect you. You must have your reasons for wanting to keep it private,' Patrick told her honestly. He knew he had no right to ask. After all, he'd kept his past to himself.

Claudia smiled at his reply. It was so refreshing in a town where everyone wanted to know everyone else's business and it somehow made her want to tell him. Many times over the weeks they had spent together she had wanted to open up but hesitated, a little scared that his opinion of her might change if he knew the truth. Then she questioned why it mattered so much what he thought of her.

'I assume it's over between you.'

'Over as soon as he discovered I was having a child.'

'Don't you mean children?'

'No, he never stayed long enough to find out I was having twins. His lawyer informed me early on that he didn't want to have his name on the birth certificate and relinquished all parental rights. He's actually...' She paused as she stumbled over her words.

'There's no need to go there,' he cut in angrily. He was furious any man would behave so poorly and sensed she was feeling torn about discussing the boys' father. 'Unless you're in witness protection and hiding from a mobster, I have no interest in knowing about a man for whom I have no respect.'

Claudia smiled. 'I'm not in witness protection.'

'That's good news then...nothing else matters.'

Claudia nodded in silence. Up until now, she had given too much thought to telling anyone, let alone Patrick, that her sons' father was a married man. *Don't do it now*, said a voice inside her head. She felt confused by her desire for him to know everything about her. 'I thought he was a good man when I met him…'

'Claudia, any man who would leave you alone and pregnant with his children is a low-life bastard. I never want to lay eyes on him. If I did I wouldn't hold back so maybe it's best I don't.' His voice was loud and filled with anger.

Claudia was taken aback. She had not seen that side of Patrick. His emotions had always seemed so moderate but hearing that reminded her of her father. She knew he would have said the same if he was still alive. Suddenly she felt more protected than she had since her parents died.

'I didn't expect that response from you.'

'I don't sit on the fence, Claudia,' he responded. 'I don't tolerate cowards or fools and the man was both.'

Claudia was compelled to confess her part in the ugly situation. She was shaking inside because she was so aware that his opinion about her might change but all of a sudden she knew she wanted to tell him anyway.

'It's more complicated than that,' she began and then paused for a moment. 'The boys' father…he was married.' The words just came tumbling out. Her heart began racing as she saw his jaw tense and his eyes become more intense.

'Married! The guy is a bigger low-life than I thought. How dare he hide that from you and disrespect his wife at the same time?'

'You're assuming I didn't know he had a wife without me saying anything?'

'Claudia, I know that you would never have become involved with a married man if you'd known he had a wife. It's not who you are. It's obvious he kept it from you.'

'He did,' she said with her head bowed a little. Patrick was visibly distraught but Claudia realised with relief that he wasn't disappointed in her. His anger was towards the man who had betrayed her. But she wanted him to know the full story. She had to take the blame for her part.

'I should have asked more questions. I was naive…'

'He was probably a seasoned cheat and wouldn't have told you the truth anyway.'

'Perhaps,' she agreed.

'This town is full of predators. I've *freshened* up a few of them. Actors, producers, agents.'

'He's a producer, quite well known in the

soap opera industry. I was working on his show and, as I said, I had absolutely no idea that he was married. He managed to hide it because his wife was away overseas, working on a remote set. She's an actress, much younger than him but not well known, not yet at least. She was apparently heading back to LA about the same time I discovered I was pregnant. He left the apartment we were sharing the day I announced we were to have a baby and I haven't heard from him since. Only his lawyer.'

Patrick ached inside to reach for her but he didn't. He didn't look at her; he stared straight ahead, scared that if he did look into her eyes he would sweep her into his arms and never let her go. It had only been nearly six weeks since they had met on the day the boys had been born but it seemed longer to Patrick. All along he'd suspected she had been hurt and now he knew by whom. The father of her children had been the one who'd inflicted the heartache.

He wanted her more than any woman he had ever met but he needed to wait until she was ready. If that never happened then so be it. But if she did open up and let him know she wanted him then he would make love to her with every fibre of his being and he would hold her in his arms all night long for as many nights as she would give him. He would try to heal every hurt she had every experienced. He would make her whole again, if she would let him.

'He'll pay the price for the rest of his life by not knowing his sons.'

Claudia opened her mouth to respond but couldn't think what to say. He had not questioned her or doubted her for a moment and she wondered how and why such a wonderful man had come into her life. Without thinking too much, she leant in to kiss his cheek but he turned his face at that moment and the softness of his lips met hers. It was an unexpected kiss but neither wanted it to end. She willingly pressed herself against his hard body. She wanted him as much as he wanted her. A welcome vulnerability washed over her as she realised how much she trusted the man she was kissing.

She trusted him more than she'd ever thought possible. And she was falling a little more in love with him by the day.

His hands trailed down the curve of her spine and she could feel his heart racing through the cool fabric of his shirt. Her heart synchronised with the beating of his and their kiss deepened as he explored her mouth. Without warning, he slowly and purposefully stood and reach for her hand to pull her up from the sofa. Once she was on her feet, he swept her up off the ground and into his arms, his mouth possessing hers again. Claudia's hands wrapped around his neck as he carried her into his bedroom, where he slowly removed every piece of her clothing. And then his own.

That night they both opened their lives, their hearts and their bodies to each other.

CHAPTER TEN

THE EARLY-MORNING SUN slipped through the gaps in the drapes and filtered onto the bed where they lay entwined in each other's arms. Claudia opened her eyes to see Patrick's handsome face only inches from hers. He was still asleep and she could feel his warm breath on her skin. Gently, she eased herself from his arms and moved to the edge of the bed in search of her clothing. It was his room, not hers, and there was no clothing in reach. Her eyes roamed the room, to find her things scattered all over the floor in a trail that led to the bed.

'Looking for something?'

She turned to see him propped up on his elbow watching her.

'My underwear.'

'I don't think you'll need that today,' he said, a spark in his eye as he pulled her back into his arms.

* * *

An hour later, Claudia woke to the smell of freshly percolated coffee. They had made love again and she had drifted into a deep and wonderful sleep. Patrick appeared in the doorway in denim jeans but no shirt. His face was freshly shaven. His hair was wet and slicked back.

'Why didn't you wake me?'

'Because, my darling, you needed your sleep.' He crossed to the bed and kissed her tenderly. 'You can have a shower and, when you're ready, there's breakfast on the patio.'

'You are spoiling me terribly.'

'I hope so,' he said as he kissed her again and she melted into his arms.

'I should get ready now,' she finally said as she pulled herself away. 'I want to be at the hospital for the boys' feed and bath.'

'Not a problem. We can eat and head over there together—it's still early.'

With that he disappeared and left her alone in the still warm bed with even warmer thoughts of him.

'There's one thing I really want to know,' she said as she traced circles with the tip of her finger on his warm bare chest and looked up lovingly at the man who had captured her heart as they sat together on the patio sofa enjoying the morning sun as they shared breakfast. She had showered quickly and they planned on being at the hospital by ten. 'Why did you really change career?'

'I found something else I enjoy—something that's rewarding and important.'

'I know, and I appreciate that you're not just fixing starlets' noses and breasts. I understand the other wonderful work you do, but you're very good at delivering babies too.'

'You only have your delivery to go on so I think your opinion may be somewhat biased.'

'There's no bias; I'm serious. You stepped in and saved us all. We owe our lives to you, Patrick.'

'You were the perfect patient...'

'Perfect patient?' She laughed and she lay back on the soft oversized outside pillow, staring at the cloudless sky as her thoughts rushed back to the day she'd given birth. It was overwhelmingly frightening sometimes when she thought about that fateful day and other times she felt so blessed and fortunate, as if the stars had aligned to place them both in the elevator. That morning, as she snuggled next to Patrick, she felt as if it must have been serendipity and she was so very lucky. 'I was perfectly horrible to you.'

'Initially, perhaps, but when labour started I think you handled yourself incredibly well. You were braver than any woman I know.'

'I don't know about the brave bit, but I do know that I was flat-out rude and chose the most inconvenient place for you to deliver the boys.'

'You didn't have much say in choosing the venue.'

'That's true…' she began but her words were cut short when his warm, soft lips pressed hard against hers and he didn't let another word escape until he had tasted her sweet mouth for the longest time.

Finally he released her. Her head was spinning, her heart was racing and it took her a moment to catch the breath he had stolen. Her thoughts about everything except the man beside her were muddled. Those thoughts were crystal-clear. She was unashamedly falling in love with him. She knew they had no certain future and they had no past, having known each other for not long over a month, but they had the present. She was falling for Patrick the way she had never fallen for a man in her life and knew she never would again.

'Let's get to the hospital and see your strapping young sons—they may have gained weight overnight and be ready to come home.'

It wouldn't be *come home*—it would be *go home*—to somewhere far away, she thought with a pang of sadness in her heart.

Claudia smiled as Patrick helped her to her feet but his words had cut like a hot blade, piercing her heart and reminding her that home for the boys and her would be London. And Patrick's home was in Los Angeles. Their brief romantic affair would be that.

Just a short, sweet affair.

As they drove to the hospital, Claudia glanced over at Patrick. His slender masculine hands that now held the steering wheel had only a few hours before been stroking her naked skin and bringing her such pleasure that she'd never wanted it to end. His profile in the morning sun was the same handsome face that had woken next to her that morning. And she hoped they would wake together every morning until she left.

But, no matter what the future held for either of them, she wanted to know more about her devilishly good-looking obstetrician. And that meant understanding the decision he had made over a decade before. She wanted to be able to answer any questions her sons might have over the years. And even if they never asked a single question, she still wanted to know all there was to know about Patrick. He was such a wonderful man, but she sensed there was something he was hiding behind the sunglasses resting on his high cheekbones, gently shaded by morning stubble. It still seemed unusual to move to the other side of the world and begin all over again. To study another medical specialty and leave behind his family and friends. To never return home when there were clearly no financial barriers was all very puzzling. And, for an inexplicable reason, she had to know what had driven him away from the country she loved.

'Patrick,' she began softly as they pulled up at traffic lights only two blocks from the Mercy Hospital. 'Can I ask you a question?'

He turned to her with a smile that melted her heart. 'It depends.'

'Depends on what?'

'Will you let me plead the Fifth Amendment if I don't like the question?'

'The Fifth Amendment? But you're not an American citizen!'

'No, I'm British—we both know that,' he

replied as he changed gear and took off as the traffic lights turned green. 'But I've been here long enough to feel comfortable using their constitutional loopholes.'

Claudia watched him smile. He was obviously trying to find a way to make light of something about his past he didn't want to discuss and his expression showed her he thought he had won.

'You know what, let's talk tonight.'

'Sounds fine to me,' he said as they drove along in the traffic heading towards the hospital.

Later, as they sat together on the patio in their swimsuits after a late-night swim, Claudia broached the subject again.

'I think you know everything there is to know about me,' she began as she ran her fingers through her wet curls to push them away from her still damp face.

'Where exactly is this going?' he asked as he began to kiss her neck where the water was trickling down from her hair. 'Because I would like to take it back to the bedroom.'

'Me too…in a minute, but first I want to take it back to the question I wanted to ask this morning.'

He stopped kissing her. 'Do we have to go there?'

'But you don't even know the question.'

'Do I really want to know? Let's leave the past where it belongs... I'm doing very nicely without it.'

Claudia sat up and turned to face Patrick. She doubted what he said was accurate. He had left everything behind. The reason had to be enormous. 'What is the deal with your family? Did you fall out?'

'I'm definitely pleading the Fifth Amendment. I told you I would this morning. Nothing's changed.'

His smile seemed forced. There was more behind it. She intended to find out exactly what. A man had once hidden a secret from her that not only changed the course of her life but that of her children. She would not and could not accept a man at face value, no matter how handsome that face.

'Patrick, I need to know a little more about you. It's important to me.' She drew a deep and slightly nervous breath. 'My cards are on the table. You know everything, good and bad, and you still want me in your bed, so please give me the same credit.'

Looking into Claudia's deep brown eyes,

Patrick felt her searching his face for answers and realised that she wasn't going to let it go. Perhaps she had a right to know. She had opened up to him about her life. Perhaps it was his turn. Maybe if she understood his reasons then she would consider staying in Los Angeles and they could be together. He suddenly had to face the truth that he had more to lose by not opening up.

He could lose Claudia.

'Fine. We are…estranged. There's been no contact with anyone from my past for close to twelve years.'

'That's sad; I couldn't imagine life with Harriet.'

'Well, I suppose that's where you and I differ then,' he said flatly. 'I can live quite nicely without my family.'

Claudia suddenly felt as if the man beside her was not the same person. How could he not want to be with his family? Family meant everything to her. Losing her parents had been a crushing blow and to think he'd just walked away from his confused her.

'Have you tried to sort out your differences?'

'This is a little deeper than simple differences. I've rebuilt my life and don't want to look back or go back. My past and my family are not relevant to me.'

As he said it he knew it wasn't the truth. Every day he thought about his family. Where his mother was, what she might be doing. His nephew would be twelve now and he had not seen him grow up and it saddened him. But there had been no other option but to walk away and let them live their lives without him.

'It's relevant to me…I mean it was significant enough to make you pack up and leave,' she replied softly. 'I don't want to open old wounds but I do want to understand you better, understand why you won't return to the place you were born.'

He stood and reached for Claudia's hand and helped her to her feet 'Then let's go inside and forget about this conversation. Just accept my past is something I don't want to relive. It will do no good. My family and I have all moved on from each other. End of story.'

Claudia lay in Patrick's arms that night but they didn't make love. Nor did she sleep well. She couldn't. It worried her that there were things in his past he wouldn't share but they were significant enough to make him leave the country he had called home, leave behind his family and never make contact again and even change his profession.

It was all so confusing.

Who was the man lying beside her? Had she made a mammoth mistake in letting him have a piece of her heart?

She climbed from bed early the next morning and had a shower before he woke. She didn't want to pry any further. Clearly he had shut down her attempts and she was not going to push him for answers. But she knew she couldn't continue to see anything between them. Honesty and openness could not be a one-way street. And while he had not promised he would open up to her, in fact he had made no promises at all, she couldn't plan a future with a man who didn't have the same values as her.

What if she and the boys did stay in LA to be a family with him and he walked away from them all and never looked back if it became too difficult? Family was everything to her and she and Harriet had already lost those they loved most. How could he not value family the way she did? To not reach out in so many years, to patch up differences and make amends—it was all incomprehensible to her.

Even if she had planned on staying in LA, it wouldn't work between them if he could place such little value on the importance of family and not explain why.

She gathered up her belongings, set them by the front door and sat on the patio and waited for him to wake.

'I'm guessing you can't leave this alone?' he said as he appeared in the doorway, dressed in shorts and a T-shirt. His expression was serious.

'No, I *can* leave it alone; in fact it's what I'm planning to do, but if I do then I have to leave us alone too. I rushed into this,' she said, shaking her head as she looked around the lovely home they had shared for over a month. 'I didn't really know you when I moved in. And I shouldn't have shared your bed for the past two nights. We're too different.'

'We're not different…'

'We're so different,' she argued. 'I would give anything to have my mother in my life. And you haven't spoken to yours in years for a reason you won't explain so I can't begin to understand. I think in time we will find more differences and I can't bring the boys into something that maybe won't last. What if you up and walk away one day and don't look back at the boys and me? My life back in London will last. My family is there. My sister. It's where I belong.'

'You don't think we have any future?'

'Not when you won't share a past that has fundamentally changed everything about who you were.'

Patrick sat down on the chair opposite her and took in a breath that filled his lungs. His long fingers ran through his hair as he looked at the ground. He realised he had no choice but to share his past or risk losing Claudia completely.

'It was almost twelve years ago,' he began without prompting. 'August seventh, to be precise.'

She remained silent but the fact that the date of his story came so easily to mind showed her just how traumatic the memory was for Patrick.

'It was a Thursday night and I took a call to assist with a high risk delivery in the county hospital where I worked in Durham,' he volunteered but the strain in his voice was obvious. 'I was an OBGYN resident and I loved what I did.'

She waited in silence for him to continue, which he did without any prompting.

'It was late, about ten o'clock, when a young woman was rushed into Emergency, presenting at the hospital in the early stages of premature labour.'

'You said you were called in; you weren't on duty then?'

'No, I had the night off. I was at the local pub with some friends from med school. It was a warm summer night; one of them had secured a placement at a hospital in New Zealand and we were giving him a send-off. Anyway, I got the call to head back. The senior obstetric consultant had left for London to speak at an OBGYN conference and couldn't get back until the next morning.'

'But if you were at the local pub you would've been drinking,' she cut in, her frown not masking her concern at the direction of his story.

He shook his head. 'Normally the answer would be yes, and by ten o'clock I would ordinarily have had a pint or two. But that night I'd finished my shift at the hospital with a bit of a headache coming on and, since I had an early start the next morning with a surgical schedule, I thought if I had even one glass of alcohol that I wouldn't pull up well. I stayed on ginger beer all night. I was perfectly fine to take the call—to be honest, I wish I had been drinking and had to refuse but I accepted and headed in to what would essentially be the end of my career in obstetrics.'

Claudia began nibbling on her lower lip. 'I still don't understand. You did nothing wrong; you hadn't been drinking...'

'I hadn't...but, with the tragedy that unfolded, some thought otherwise. That was the only conclusion they could find for what happened in the operating theatre. They couldn't accept that a high risk pregnancy extends to a high risk delivery. Anyway, I scrubbed in and began the Caesarean, but very cautiously as there was a complication, as I mentioned. The placenta was growing outside of the uterus wall and, despite me doing everything textbook and taking precautions along the way, the patient began to haemorrhage. I lifted the baby boy clear of the womb but as there was so much blood I couldn't see where to begin the repair. The blood loss was too great and, despite the whole team doing everything we could, we lost her on the table. There was nothing I, or anyone, could do. The theatre staff knew I had done everything right and told me as much but the jury were sitting outside in the waiting room and, to be honest, the worst juror was myself. I took the blame before I saw them—they just reinforced my feelings.'

'Why would you do that? You knew it wasn't your fault and the medical team knew it wasn't...'

'For me, overwhelming guilt that I had not been able to save her and, for them, their own grief turned to anger when they were told I had been seen having *drinks* at the local only an hour before. It cemented it in the minds of the family that I had to have been drinking and that was why their little girl died giving birth.'

'Why didn't you fight? Surely there must have been something you could have done? It's so unfair that you did the right thing in returning to the hospital and you tried to save the woman and you had the family blame you on circumstantial evidence.'

'It shattered my world. I was grieving too, and they needed someone to blame for the loss of her life. I decided it was my duty to take that blame.' Patrick paused and stared at Claudia thoughtfully and in silence for a moment. He didn't want to tell her any more.

He had omitted the most important fact in the entire tragedy. The one that had changed his life completely. But he had to be honest. She deserved to know the truth.

With a heavy heart, he closed his eyes. 'The young woman who died...was my sister.'

CHAPTER ELEVEN

'YOUR SISTER DIED having her baby?'

He nodded, unable to bring himself to say the words again.

'So it was your own family that blamed you? It's so sad that she died, but why would they do that? I don't understand—families don't do that to each other.'

'It's not their fault. It was complicated,' he said, trying to validate their behaviour. 'No one knew Francine, or Franny, as we always called her growing up, was a high risk so to them her death had to be due to negligence.'

'Surely your brother-in-law knew there were complications?'

'No, he had no idea.' Patrick shook his head. 'I assume she kept her medical condition from us because she didn't want anyone to worry. We had just endured another tragedy a few months before, so she was trying to protect everyone.'

'What sort of tragedy?'

'My younger brother, Matthew, died six months before.'

Claudia covered her mouth with her hands as she gasped, 'Oh, no.'

'My father and mother had divorced a long time before; I was young when it happened. My mother raised us. One Saturday my mother went up to Matthew's room to wake him as he had friends waiting downstairs to head to Brighton for the day. She found him in bed, which was unusual since he was an early riser. She patted his legs to wake him, but my brother was unresponsive so she pulled the covers down and found he was bleeding from the nose and mouth. My mother called out for help from his friends and dialled for an ambulance, hoping the paramedics would somehow revive him. They couldn't and he was pronounced dead on arrival at the hospital.' Patrick's jaw was clenched and Claudia could see he was struggling to make eye contact.

Claudia's brow was knitted in confusion. She wondered if it might have been a drug

nant. It brought some joy back to our mother and to our family. She was focusing on the new baby on the way and I don't think that Franny wanted to bring her down with worry. She wanted her to hold on to something. The thought of a baby arriving gave us all a light at the end of the tunnel. We knew she was having a boy, that part she shared, and in some way I think the fact another boy would join the family made losing Matthew *almost* bearable for our mother. I'm assuming Franny didn't want our mother to be anxious and, while I understand her wanting to protect her, she should have confided in me. I could have ensured the best antenatal care and would have been prepared, going into surgery.'

'So she never took her husband to any of her obstetric visits?'

'No, Will never attended any of them.'

'Still, whether they knew or not, I can't believe they would blame you.'

'They didn't understand, even when I explained that her medical condition translated into a high risk delivery.'

'But, without any medical knowledge, it still doesn't make sense to throw the blame your way; it all seems unfair and so wrong.'

'Don't forget I'd been seen in the pub; they

forgot everything about her condition and focused purely on my supposed drinking.'

'But you hadn't been drinking. Couldn't you have a blood test and prove it?'

'I didn't think to have the test the night she died as, since I hadn't been drinking, it didn't cross my mind to cover myself and the allegations came out the next day from my brother-in-law's family. One of his cousins had seen me at the pub and, despite me telling them otherwise, they didn't believe that I had been completely sober.'

'But couldn't your friends corroborate your story?'

Patrick nodded. 'They tried, but his family was convinced it was just my medico mates covering for me. The whole medical fraternity banding together to protect each other conspiracy theory.'

'And your brother-in-law believed them?'

'He was upset, he was half out of his mind and he got swept up in the witch hunt. There was even footage taken on a mobile phone of another celebration in which I featured in the background. It was all over. You have to remember I lost my sister that day. I couldn't argue in my frame of mind. I was grieving too.'

'What about the rest of your family? Your mother and father?' Claudia frowned in perplexity. It all seemed so wrong.

'My mother was barely functioning and she believed what she was told. My negligence had taken away her beloved daughter.'

'But you had tried to save your sister, with no knowledge of her medical condition…and I know it couldn't bring her daughter back, but she had a grandchild. The grandchild that you had brought into the world.'

Patrick ran his hands through his hair in frustration. 'I was hung, drawn and quartered by the town. There was no coming back from that so I left. It was best for everyone.'

'Are you sure about that?'

'The grief blanketed both families and I guess I just couldn't face the arguing. I made the decision to leave. If either family wanted to look into it further I left the name of her obstetrician, but they never called. They didn't want to look further than me for the cause. It was their choice to direct the blame at me and it was my choice to walk away.'

'It's all so terribly unfair.'

'Yes, but it's done.'

'And your brother-in-law and his son…?'

'Will named the little boy Todd after his

father. Todd turned twelve this August. He's a tall boy like his father and doing well at school.'

'So you speak with your brother-in-law then?'

'No, I haven't heard a word from him since I left. A friend from university lives not far from him; their boys go to the same school. He keeps an eye out for them and keeps me up to date. I set up a trust fund to cover his college education. Will gave up work for a period to raise Todd and then found it hard to get back into the workforce so had to start again at entry level. I feel I owed him to take care of Todd.

'So now you can understand why I choose to live over here. It's simpler for everyone.'

Claudia saw everything so differently. 'While I understand your need to leave, and I think what happened to you is almost unforgivable, it's still your family. You can't turn your back on family. Your mother lost her daughter and both sons within months of each other.'

'I'm still here. I didn't die.'

'No, but you left her life. For a mother it would be the same level of grief.'

Patrick leaned back against the chair. 'No,

it's not the same. I'm here but she chose not to contact me. Nor did Will.'

'Perhaps your absence cemented their doubts about what happened. You could have gone back anytime over the last twelve years and cleared it up.'

'I'm not about to stir up all that again. I have built a new life here and reconstructive surgery has been good to me.'

'So you gave up obstetrics because you couldn't save your sister.'

'Yes,' he said solemnly and without hesitation. 'I had nightmares about her lying lifeless on the table at my hands…I lost the will and drive to practice.'

'But it wasn't because of anything you did.'

Patrick felt his body tense. 'I couldn't face that sense of helplessness again. Being unable to save Franny was something I could not relive.'

'But you did…with me. And you saved me. You didn't know I had a serious condition and you saved me from dying.'

'No, the paramedics came in time to save you.'

Her face became even more serious. 'They took over but you had kept me alive.'

Patrick knew the best thing he had done

was to walk away from obstetrics and his family. And he knew that Claudia was testing that resolve. 'Fine, I kept you alive but I can't go back to that. I'm content with my work. I live here now and I'll never set foot back in the UK.'

'But your work here, now, it's not your first love.'

'No, but you can't always have everything you want, Claudia, including your first love.'

She couldn't ignore the resolve in Patrick's voice. 'Have you never thought about returning to Durham and facing your accusers and telling the truth?'

Patrick rolled his eyes and did not hide his exasperation. 'There was no evidence. Nothing to support me and everything to support their accusations.'

She shrugged. 'But you walked away from your career…and your life…because of lies.'

Patrick's body went rigid and his voice became harsh. 'I didn't walk away from anything. I left to make it easier for everyone.'

'Why can't you face the past now then? Rebuild your life in London? It was twelve years ago and I'm sure your mother would give anything to hold you in her arms again. You're her only living child.'

'No. I can't and I won't go back. My life there is over. It ended the day I left.'

Gaping at him, Claudia exclaimed, 'That's so dramatic!'

'My sister died, Claudia. They all think I caused her death. *That* is dramatic.'

Claudia frowned at him while she scrutinised his face. His expression was severe. His jaw appeared more pronounced. 'I'm just saying perhaps you could explain it properly. Have your peers explain it again. Franny's obstetrician could sit down with your mother and tell her the truth. It would have been near on impossible for your mother to pick up the telephone and speak with him. But you could facilitate that conversation. Make her see reason. Would that be so hard for you to do?'

'It's too late. They've moved on with their lives.'

'It's never too late. No mother moves on from a child.'

'I'm not so sure.'

'I am. I couldn't imagine a day without Thomas and Luca in my life. I would travel to the end of the earth to be with them and you should do the same for your nephew. You've chosen to give up without a fight.'

'Fighting is overrated.'

'Not in my books. I need a man who will fight for family.'

Patrick stood up and crossed back to the doorway. His face was taut as he knew at that moment exactly how Claudia felt.

Claudia sat staring ahead. Her heart was aching with the reality that had just been spelt out to her. 'It's been a long time and your mother would probably be stronger now. Don't you think you owe it to her to let her know what really happened? I would want to know.'

'Claudia, let it go.'

'You mean let us go?'

He rubbed his clenched jaw. Claudia noticed his eyes suddenly looked tired, almost battle-worn as he spoke. 'The choice is yours.'

CHAPTER TWELVE

PATRICK STIRRED FROM a tortured sleep the next morning, knowing that his every reason for waking up was gone. Claudia had left. She had grabbed her belongings and caught a cab. She'd told him where she would be staying if he changed his mind and wanted to talk but he left the slip of paper by the bed. He had no intention of calling. She was right—she deserved to be with Harriet. Family was important to her. He had learned to get along on his own for a long time. He missed his mother and his brother-in-law and wished with all of his heart some days that he could be there to watch his nephew grow up. But he couldn't. The wounds had healed on the outside and he didn't want to rip them open by travelling home.

It was better to let her rebuild her life back

in the UK. She would settle in quickly and no doubt move on.

She would forget about what they'd shared in time and someone else would take his place.

But he wasn't sure he would ever move on.

Claudia had brought more joy and happiness into his life than he had dreamt possible. She was everything he could wish for in a woman and more. And he had let her walk away.

He had never felt so empty and it filled him with regret to walk away from Claudia but there was no other choice. What she expected from him was impossible. How could he face his family again? Where would he start? Would the blame still be there? The desolation in his mother's eyes—so empty, so blank, so lost and hurt by him that he could never go back. He just couldn't. It was better to leave the past behind.

When he'd discovered she had left that morning he had tried to push what they had shared from his mind but, waking on the second day, it became a reality. And he could no longer ignore the way he felt. A cloud had moved over his world and it was suddenly a much darker place, devoid of everything he had come to love.

Glancing around the room, his eyes came to rest on the bedside table, where the framed photos of Thomas and Luca were resting. It was the first time she had reached out to him and let him into her world. He now knew how difficult that had been for her but she had fought her doubts and insecurities, and waded through the hurt, to let him know that he meant something to her and the boys.

Next to the photographs was the note she had left—and her pearl earrings.

A rush of memories assailed his mind.

The day they'd met in the elevator. How beautiful he'd thought Claudia was and how he'd quickly discovered her looks were matched with her feisty spirit. She was a strong woman on the outside but inside she was filled with love. That day he had witnessed the level of that love for her sons and, weeks later, experienced first-hand her capacity for love when she'd shared his bed.

And he had let her leave.

Perhaps she was right. He had taken the easier option. But that suited him. He had adjusted to the values in the city. At least that was what he would have to tell himself. He climbed from bed and headed for the shower. He had the day off and no idea how to spend it. Claudia was gone and he couldn't visit Thomas and Luca. He had to become accustomed to life without them and that wouldn't happen if he tried to reach out to them even one last time.

After a quick shower, he dressed in a polo shirt and jeans and, looking for something to occupy his mind, he decided to head to his practice. His hair was still wet and he was unshaven but he knew he wouldn't be seeing anyone at that hour. There had to be some paperwork to finish, reports to finalise and mail to check. Anything to stop him rethinking the decision he had made.

As he entered the garage he looked at the SUV that Claudia had been driving and made a mental note to call a dealership and trade it in. He didn't want to be reminded of what he had lost every time he saw the car that he now considered to be hers.

There was little traffic that early in the morning and he was at work in less than ten minutes. The cleaner was leaving as he pulled into the undercover car park; they acknowledged each other with a wave before the young man climbed into his van and left.

Patrick took the stairwell to his first floor office. It was empty and quiet. So quiet that his own thoughts were almost deafening. He wished the cleaner had stayed so the sound of the vacuum could drown out the doubts that were pounding inside his head.

He rifled through the papers on his desk and then noticed the pile of mail that his receptionist had sorted and put aside as not urgent. He hadn't looked at it for a few weeks but he trusted Anita would have brought anything important to his attention.

He read them one by one but nothing brought even a hint of enthusiasm to him. There was an invitation to attend a benefit for the Screen Actors Guild at the Beverly Wilshire; an invitation to drive a new luxury sedan that had arrived at a dealership in Santa Monica; a bi-monthly magazine from the Cosmetic Surgeons of America and numerous professional association offers and advertisements. It was all as he'd expected.

Then he spied a gift certificate from an expensive women's store on Rodeo Drive; it was only three doors down from his practice. He picked up the beautifully presented certificate and noticed it was for a sizeable amount. He wondered if they had made a mistake sending it to him, then he froze. This was the same store where his receptionist had ordered some pyjamas and toiletries for Claudia all those weeks ago. But why would they be sending him a gift certificate? It was far too generous to be a thank you in return for his business. He turned it over and found a note on the back.

Dear Dr Spencer
Miss Monticello insisted that she repay the kindness of the 'anonymous' customer. We did not reveal your details; however, she insisted that she provide a certificate of equal value to you. We hope a lovely lady in your life can enjoy shopping in our store in the near future.
Warmest regards
Camille and staff

He closed his eyes and dropped his head back to look up at the ceiling. He knew he had to be the most stupid man in the world. She still had no idea that he had sent the parcel. She'd just wanted to repay a stranger. She could have just walked away but she had so much pride and honesty she had found a way to return what she didn't feel in her heart was hers. In a city of people who were only too willing to take, Claudia wanted only to give. And he knew she would have struggled to have covered the cost. She had so little money but she still did the right thing. She never let her values slip or chose the easy way out.

She'd fought so hard to bring her boys into the world. She never gave up on who or what she loved, no matter what obstacles she faced.

Claudia was an amazing, wonderful woman and he had just let her go.

She had dropped her walls, despite all the disappointment she had endured; she had let him into her life and her heart, and how had he repaid her? He had been as cruel as the father of her children. Perhaps even worse, he berated himself, because he knew what Claudia had been through. And she had allowed him to become a part of her babies' lives.

His head was upright as he stared at the door. His jaw flicked with mounting fury. At himself and the lies that had changed his life. He drew breath and filled his lungs, and suddenly felt adrenaline rush through his body.

He wouldn't let it happen again. Walking away from a life with Claudia, Thomas and Luca was not what he wanted to do. Not now, not ever. He wasn't sure he deserved them but he knew he wanted to fight to have them in his life. The thought of the boys' birth certificates having no father listed made him want even more to be the father figure in their lives. To guide them and to love them. If Claudia would let him, he would willingly take on that role. Forever.

He knew that meant reconciling with his family, no matter how difficult that might be. Perhaps time had healed some wounds, perhaps not. But Patrick wasn't about to base his future on assumptions. He would visit and see first-hand. And if they didn't want him back, then he would accept it but he wouldn't run away. He wanted a life back in London with Claudia...if she would have him.

He threw down the certificate and raced from the office. He had to prove to Claudia that he would fight for her and her boys and their future. He would do whatever it took. It was time to take a stand.

There was just one thing he had to do before he left to find her—he had a flight to book to London.

Claudia had packed her suitcase and left it by the door for the concierge to collect as she made her way to the hotel lobby to check out. Her tears had finally dried. She told herself firmly that Patrick Spencer would be the last man she would waste precious tears on. She would concentrate on raising her sons and forget about any other love. Her boys would be enough to fill her life and she knew they would never let her down. And, more importantly, she would never let them down. She would be there for them and give them everything they needed, growing up. And she hoped one day as grown men each would find their true love and she would be happy for them.

With a sigh for what might have been, she approached the reception desk.

'Good morning, Miss Monticello, are you checking out today?'

The young woman was dressed in a corporate charcoal suit, tortoiseshell glasses and a pleasant but predictable smile. Her hair was pulled back in a sleek chignon.

'Yes, I am. Can you please add a bottle of lemonade I took from the minibar to my credit card along with the room charges? I was staying in Room 303.'

The receptionist checked the computer screen and handed over the account.

Claudia passed over her credit card then tucked her hair behind her ear as she stood waiting for the card to be processed. She felt for her pearl earring, the way she always did when she was nervous. But it wasn't there. Her hand switched to the other ear. That one was missing too. She hadn't even thought about them for two days. Her head had been filled with thoughts so much more demanding of her time than her jewellery. She suddenly remembered she had left them on the bedside table. Patrick's bedside table.

'Are you looking for these?'

Claudia spun around to find a dishevelled Patrick standing behind her, her earrings in his outstretched hand.

'I would like to speak with Miss Monticello in private,' Patrick told the young woman at the desk, now looking at both of them. 'Do you have a room available?'

'The business centre has some private meeting rooms,' the receptionist told them, adjusting her glasses. 'You're more than welcome to use one of those.'

'Thank you,' Patrick replied, glancing around the lobby and spying the business centre.

'There's no need to thank her; we won't be using the room,' Claudia retorted, shaking her head in defiance. 'There's nothing I need or want to say to you, Patrick. I'm leaving today. We're over.'

'There's so much I want to say to you and I'd like to say it in private.'

With a look of discomfort Claudia felt certain was due to the potential for a situation to play out in her lobby, the receptionist interrupted. 'As I said, you're both more than welcome to use any of the meeting rooms and at this hour they're all free.'

Patrick led the way and crossed the lobby foyer with long purposeful strides and waited by the door of the business centre for Claudia's response. In silence she begrudgingly walked up to him. With each step across the large Mexican-inspired tiled floor of the lobby, the ache in her heart made her more resolute in her decision to end this meeting as soon as possible and never see Patrick again. She was angry and hurt in equal proportions that he had made her so vulnerable. She would hear him out then leave before she weakened and let her heart tell her what to do. She couldn't live her life with a man who had such different values to her own.

He softly closed the door behind them. 'I've got so much to say to you, Claudia, and it begins with an apology.'

'There's no point. I don't want an apology.'

'But you deserve one. I should never have let you walk out of my life and I apologise for that. I've been the biggest fool and you were right. I need to fight for what's important. That's you *and* my family. Claudia, I don't want to lose you and I'll do whatever it takes for us to be together, if you'll let me.'

'What do you mean *if I'll let you*?' she demanded. 'What are you telling me?'

'I want a life with you and your sons.'

'I can't stay here in LA; I told you that.'

'I know that and I wouldn't want you to stay here,' he said, taking her hands in his. 'I want to come home with you. I want to go back to London and do what you made me realise I should have done years ago. I want to set things right with my family. At least try to anyway.'

Claudia didn't pull her hands free as her expression turned from confusion to something closer to joy. 'Are you really serious about that?'

'I've never been more serious.'

'But why now? What's changed in two days?'

'I had time to think. Time to miss you and realise it's something I should have done a long time ago. Because I don't want to lose you or the boys.'

'And when are you planning on doing this?' Her voice did not betray the happiness she felt building inside. She did not dare to allow herself to believe he wanted a life with her, only to be disappointed again.

'As soon as I can sell the practice, I will move home to the UK permanently. You're right, my first love has always been obstetrics. And I can do it. I can honour my sister's life and her bravery by bringing more children into the world, not trying to forget what happened.'

'You really want to go back to what you had before?'

'It won't be exactly what I had before. So much has changed, but I will deal with everything if I have you in my life.'

'This is a huge commitment to change everything about the life you lead. It's a big adjustment.'

'And it's one I need to make.'

'Then I will see you when you arrive,' she said, hoping with all of her heart that it wasn't an empty promise. She had become a realist and knew it might take time to sell the practice. In that time he might change his mind.

overdose but she said nothing. Asking such a question seemed cruel and unnecessary. The details made no difference. Patrick had tragically lost his younger brother.

'The autopsy report from the coroner's office came back with suspected lung aneurism,' Patrick offered without prompting. 'In simple terms, it's a ruptured artery in the lungs, which meant he drowned in his own blood. It's extremely rare and nothing that could have been predicted. Matthew had been a medical time bomb for a very long time.'

'I'm so sorry.' Claudia couldn't find any other words. Nothing she thought to say seemed to be adequate for the tragedy she had heard. His family had been dealt an overwhelmingly sad time.

'It was the worst time in my mother's life, in all of our lives. My father attended the funeral but after that he kept his distance again. My maternal grandmother was alive, but only barely, as she was living in assisted care; the shock of the broken marriage was difficult but hearing that her grandson had died was what I believe sent her into a depression that she never really recovered from.

'Then Franny discovered she was preg-

'You will see me sooner than that. I'll be travelling with you in about four hours' time,' he told her as he looked at his watch. 'You'll need help with the boys on the long haul flight…and to settle into your home.'

'You're travelling from LAX to Heathrow with me tonight?'

He pulled the airline ticket from his back trouser pocket. 'If you'll let me.'

Claudia smiled in return and immediately felt herself being pulled into Patrick's strong embrace and his lips pressed tenderly against hers. He pulled back for a moment to look lovingly into her eyes.

'I love you, Claudia Monticello, more than I ever have or ever will love anyone and more than I thought possible. You've given me the reason and strength to fight for what I want. Don't doubt, even for a moment, that you're my reason for waking up every day because that is what you've become. I don't want to live without you and if you'll marry me you will make me the happiest man in the world.'

Tears of happiness welled in her eyes as she nodded. 'Of course I'll marry you, Dr Spencer.'

EPILOGUE

'DADDY!' CRIED THOMAS and Luca in unison as they ran to greet Patrick.

Thomas was a little taller than Luca but they both had mops of thick black hair and smiles as wide as their chubby, and slightly ruddy, little faces.

'How was your first day at school?' he asked as he scooped both of the boys into his strong grip, resting one child on each hip as they wrapped their little arms around him. 'Did you enjoy it?'

'I like it home with Mummy and you better,' said Luca and he nestled his head onto Patrick's broad shoulder.

'Me too, Daddy,' Thomas agreed. 'But there's a turtle in the classroom so it'th not too bad.'

'Yeth, I like the turtle very much.' Luca lifted his head from Patrick's shoulder and chimed in. 'I think I might ask Father Christmas for one.'

'And Mummy got some of your favourite toffee from the lolly shop today too,' Thomas exclaimed. 'The special one with the yummy chocolate all over it.'

Just then, Claudia walked down the hallway of the beautiful Knightsbridge townhouse they had called home for almost five years and a smile spread over Patrick's face. She looked as stunning as she had the day they married and he loved the thoughtful things she did, like buying his favourite chocolate-covered almond toffee and kissing him every day, the same way she had done the very first time. He placed the boys both down on their feet again and ruffled their hair with his hands before they ran off to play outside.

'And how was your day, darling?' she asked as she threw her arms around Patrick's neck and kissed him.

'Not too bad, but it just became much, much better,' he told her as he kissed her tenderly and pulled her closer to him.

Claudia held her body against his, relishing the warmth of his embrace. Every morning she woke in his arms and fell a little more in love with the man who had made her believe in love again.

'Did you deliver any gorgeous babies today?'

'Two, actually,' he replied with a proud grin. 'And I'm inducing one of my IVF patients tomorrow morning. She's overdue, so she's been admitted to hospital this afternoon. The whole family is on standby and very excited.'

'Well, my day was wonderful too. Harriet and Matteo have finished renovations on their kitchen and want us over for an early dinner on Saturday. Matteo built a sandpit for the twins so the four of them can get messy together.'

'Sounds great. Matteo's quite the handyman. Perhaps he can help me to build one for the boys.'

'Oh, and Will called and he's coming over on Sunday with Todd and your mother for a roast. Todd's looking at universities for the year after next and wants your advice. His heart's set on studying medicine like his uncle. Thinks he wants to specialise in OBGYN.'

'Well, I'll do my best to talk him out of that.'

'You'll do no such thing. Where would I

be today if you hadn't studied obstetrics?' she argued playfully. 'Just tell him to always have his medical bag handy when travelling in elevators and be prepared for anything if there's a pregnant woman in there with him.'

'Even falling in love.'

'Yes, even falling in love,' Claudia replied as she looked lovingly at her husband.

He pulled her close to him and kissed her again. 'Did I ever tell you that I am the luckiest man in the world and that I couldn't possibly love you any more than I do now?'

'You haven't told me today, Dr Spencer,' she said, running her fingers lightly down his chest. 'But you have mentioned it once or twice over the years.'

'Once or twice?' He laughed as his hands slipped down her spine and rested on the curve of her bottom. 'Well, just so you know how much, I will show you, Mrs Spencer. Once the sun has set and our boys are in bed, of course.'

She kissed him again and, hand in hand, they walked down the hall, both hoping the sun would set early that night.

And every night for the rest of their lives.

* * * * *

If you missed the first story in
THE MONTICELLO BABY MIRACLES
duet check out
ONE NIGHT, TWIN CONSEQUENCES
by Annie O'Neil

*And if you enjoyed this story, check out
these other great reads from
Susanne Hampton*

*A MUMMY TO MAKE CHRISTMAS
A BABY TO BIND THEM
FALLING FOR DR DECEMBER
BACK IN HER HUSBAND'S ARMS*

All available now!